The Exile's Gift

Sharon Skinner

Brick Cave Media
brickcavebooks.com
2019

Cover Illustration by Thitipon Decruen
xric7

Brick Cave Media
brickcavebooks.com
2019

To Ciara.

Thank you for being the first to bring Kira to life.

The Exile's Gift

Sharon Skinner

Brick Cave Media
brickcavebooks.com

Chapter 1

"Kira," Milos murmured, his warm breath tickling her ear.

Kira smiled and rolled toward him, reaching to embrace him, but he was too far away, the bedding beside her cold to the touch. She opened her eyes to find herself alone, and the sharp-edged loss drove itself into her heart once more.

She wiped a hand across her eyes. Pale dawn light seeped in through the shuttered window. At the foot of the bed, Kelmir lay curled, his lavender eyes watching her. His stillness might unnerve another, but Kira was used to the big hunting cat's quietude and knew it didn't mean he wasn't alert and able to spring to action without warning should the need arise.

Not that there should be need here in her stately bedchamber.

From the great arched fireplace to the artistically woven draperies and rugs, the room reeked of comfort and privilege to which she was unaccustomed. How much more she would have preferred the damp hold of a small ship, or even an open camp in a forest clearing, any place else, as long as it was with Milos.

Perched upon the bedpost, Vaith stretched his neck and unfurled his leathery wings before hopping down onto the pillow beside her, thankfully pulling her away from such thoughts.

"Good morning, my little wyvern princeling," she murmured. He tilted his head to the side and turned a golden eye on her. When she didn't move, he slid his head under her hand in an effort to get her to stroke his long neck. She ran her fingers along his spine, his cool scales a familiar comfort. "You're a pushy little prince, this morning."

Kelmir yawned and let out a low rumble as if to suggest this morning was no different than any other. With a flick of his tail, he leaped from the bed to the floor, arched his back and stretched.

Kira sighed. No. Despite the morning ritual with Vaith and Kelmir, this morning *was* different. Would be *very* different. This was the morning the Gilded Hawk would leave the shores of Eilar, taking the Aestron sailors back home.

And with them, Milos.

Sorrow and anger warred inside her. She hadn't seen him since that day in the palace garden. The day she had offered him a place beside her. The day he had refused her offer to remain, to take a seat upon the Guardian's dais as her consort. The day he had turned from her and walked away.

True, she had been as stubborn as he, refusing to go with him, yet not fully explaining why. Oh, she had shared her need to help her people, her commitment to the land, all of which was true. But she had not told him of her inheritance, the connection to this land that had been passed on to her. The tie to the land that pulled at her even now, as if every movement was either buoyed up or anchored down by the ropy energy that crisscrossed the land beneath her feet. A tie bequeathed to Kira by the dying Matriarch during their struggle with her half brother, Kavyn.

The Matriarch.

The woman every Eilaran believed to be Kira's mother. The woman who had mourned her and then refused to claim her. A woman who had traded a dead heir for a living child, even though that child symbolized a heart's betrayal. Kira still hadn't shared that dark secret with anyone. How could she? How could she tell the people of this island that the bloodline of the Guardians, their protectors for generations, had been as good as severed?

And how could she explain what had happened in the Guardian's room between her, the Matriarch and her half-brother? She herself still didn't truly understand the so-called gift the Matriarch had bestowed upon her. Nor would she know how to explain why she had not confessed all of this to the Council immediately.

What had she truly feared? That they would simply accept her as their Matriarch? Or that they would believe her and find a way to remove from her the tie to the land? And why did both possibilities send such trembles through her?

She shoved back the coverlet and sat up, the weight of what she had done, what she had become, making it difficult to rise. But rise she must. There were matters to see to. And, with Matriarch Kyrina gone and Kavyn no more than a blubbering wreck, Kira was now, for better or worse, the one who must see to them.

Sitting on the edge of the bed, she hesitated, the heat of the bedding luring her, urging her to lie back down, to let all of the responsibilities take care of themselves, let all the worry wait, let go the burdens that threatened to fall so heavily upon her shoulders.

She toyed with the idea. Why not push things off one more day? Surely, there was no official limit to how long one could mourn such a great loss. Not that she could tell anyone that her sorrow lay more with the leaving of a certain ship than the death of her presumed mother.

She wondered at her new-found ability to make excuses for herself. She'd never been one to shirk her duties. Well, except for that period of rebelliousness with Heresta. And that time in her life had caused great sorrow, both for her mentor and herself. The choices she had made had led to so much pain and suffering. Yet, had she not chosen that path, she would not have met Milos. Though, as much as she hated to think it, perhaps that would have been for the better.

You are who you are because of your choices, Heresta's voice whispered in her head. *You cannot walk another's path.*

But this path seemed such a chore. Her body felt ponderous, her heart heavy. Even her face seemed pulled, as if her physical self was being drawn downward. Not the attraction of the lines, exactly. She'd become accustomed to that pull of power. This was something else that she couldn't quite fathom. As if night were already falling again—though the sun had barely risen on a new day—draining her vitality.

A light rap at her chamber door stopped her from slipping back under the inviting covers.

With a sigh, she slipped her arms into the sleeves of her dressing robe and tied it around her as she stood, bare feet sinking into the soft rugs, and crossed the room to unlatch the door.

The lock was new, an addition she had made to the Matriarch's chamber once she had been convinced to move into the room.

Room. She swept another gaze around her before opening the door. It was more like a small palace of its own, nestled within the Guardian's Keep. It made her feel insignificant and even more out of place than she had when she had first come to Eilar. No easy feat.

She let the door swing inward and found herself face-to-face, not with one of the Matriarch's care-taking staff, nor Kelliss, the young Physic's apprentice, but with the Physica Devira herself. The older woman stood outside the room, hands resting within her robes, a habit she had adopted after her hands had been injured, scarred by an angry outburst of the past Matriarch upon the discovery of her consort's assassination and the kidnapping of her only daughter.

Which was also a lie.

The revelation that she was not the Matriarch's true heir still weighed heavily on Kira. She wondered for at least the thousandth time if she should not simply tell the Council the truth, run to the docks and leave on the Gilded Hawk with Milos as her heart urged her to.

But she knew she could not abandon the island and leave its people defenseless. Nor could she go without helping them to discover what was causing the illness that lost them their powers and had cost the lives of so many of their most gifted children.

No. She must find a way to help heal this land and bring back the balance she had helped to destroy during the conflict with her half-brother. And who knew what attempting to leave might do to both her and the land?

"Matriarch?" Devira still stood in the hallway, waiting to be acknowledged.

"My apologies," Kira told her, stepping aside and waving the Physica into the room. "My mind was wandering again." As if it did anything else. "My sleep was restless. Please forgive me."

"There is nothing to forgive. It is early, the sun practically still sleeping, as we begin our work, and I must beg your forgiveness for the disturbance, but I felt the need to speak with you. And, as I was sleepless myself, I found my footsteps leading me to your door." Devira limped into the room, her body still not healed from the tumble she had taken when Kavyn had shoved her down the steps of the Matriarch's dais. The Physics had done their best, but the fall had nearly killed the poor woman, and had left her further crippled, likely for the rest of her life. It was a miracle she was up and moving, at all.

"Please, have a seat while I stir the fire," Kira said, keenly aware of the woman's stiff movement. "Are you well?" She hoped it would pass as a proper way to ask after Devira's health without being rude. "This early, there is no morning repast at hand. Yet, I can offer you tea."

"Thank you for the consideration. I'll take a seat, but please, don't trouble yourself about the fire. Or the tea. Unless you do so for your own comfort." Devira waved her off with a gnarled hand, slowly lowering her stiff body into a padded chair beside the hearth. "Your other question is a thin disguise for wondering if my recent injuries are healing properly," Devira said, shooting Kira a piercing look.

Kira opened her mouth to object, but Devira cut her off. "The answer is yes. I am well tended and cared for in that regard. It pays to be a mentor in the house of healing." She gave Kira a tight smile. "My sleeplessness is due more to the fact that I am simply still unused to sleeping in the healer's quarters. My old body misses my...own bed." She closed her mouth into a stiff line, as if she would liked to have bitten off the words rather than letting them escape her lips.

Kira nodded in understanding. She knew that what Devira truly missed was not her bed, but rather the person she had shared it with for so many turns. Devira had separated herself from her lifemate, Zoshia, at about the same time Kira had parted ways with Milos. She wondered what had driven them apart. Was it duty, as with her, or something more personal?

The two women sat in silence for a few moments. Clearly, Kira was not the only one facing difficulties in adjusting to the change in her relationship status. Neither of them, it seemed, was completely happy with their current situation.

"Well, that's enough brooding for one day." Devira finally broke the silence. "I have heard that the Council grows impatient with our new Guardian." She tucked her hands inside her sleeves as she spoke. "You have them at a loss."

"I have been more than clear with the Council," Kira said, shoving her icy toes beneath a thick foot rug. She leaned forward and used the metal poker to prod the dying coals into flame.

"Indeed, you have," Devira said. "But clarity of language is not the same as clarity of purpose. They wish to know why you have accepted the title of Matriarch, yet refuse to perform the Guardian's ritual and assume your position in earnest."

Kira shivered thinking of the cold stone seat and the recent battle that had taken place within the Guardian's room. Not to mention the revelations made during that altercation. And her new status as both heir and liar. "You know why." She settled the last of the kindling onto the coals, then sat back, folding her arms across her chest and wishing she could tell Devira everything. What would the older woman think of her, if she knew she was not truly the Matriarch's heir? She had put so much faith in Kira, in the good she might do for her people. Kira stared down at the floor to hide the guilt that felt painted onto her skin.

"I make no assumptions in the regard to your motives, nor am I here to chastise you." Devira held her withered fingers out to the flickering blaze. "Ancestors know, there are enough thoughts being voiced on the matter without mine added in."

Kira gathered that the sharpness in the statement was directed at someone, though she was uncertain whom it might be. "I've told you," she said, trying not to let her frustration color her voice, "what happened between Kavyn and myself, the shattering of that talisman of his and... the death of the Matriarch..." She shifted in her seat and leaned forward and lowered her voice to a barely audible whisper. "Between Physica and patient, the Guardian's seat repels me." Her phrasing was deliberate, designed to ensureDevira would be unable to divulge her confession. The rules of confidentiality were tantamount to the woman's profession. There was truth in her admission of the revulsion the stone seat caused in her, but Kira also hoped that expressing her feelings on the matter would be enough to still the pressure of being pushed into a role for which she felt totally unprepared. Not to mention the fear that she might be somehow revealed as an imposter should she take up the true mantle of the Matriarch and all of its trappings. No, she needed to tread carefully here. At least until she better understood the power the Matriarch had imbued her with.

"I have considered what you told me of the events that took place in the Guardian's Room, and I admit I still have no answers. Nor do I have much recollection aside from attempting to shield our Matriarch and then finding myself in the house of healing. I have, however, requested Aertine to examine the shards of Kavyn's power stone. I hope with the aid of her extensive skills, we may be able to discern its full purpose. And perhaps from whence it came."

Kira stiffened, glancing up at the Physica. "But I haven't even told the Council the full extent of what Kavyn seemed to be capable of by virtue of using it. Should they discover the power it wielded..." She didn't like the images that welled up at the thought of someone replicating the stone. She had only been able to stop Kavyn with the help of the Matriarch. Should she have to face alone another person so armed... Dread placed a heavy hand upon her shoulder at the thought. She clutched the armrests of the chair until her hands hurt. "I entrusted you with its keeping only because I could not fathom it on my own. The powers that rule here, that rule that object are still...foreign to me." Her whispered words rasped with the hard-edged anger that ground them out. The web of power that lay upon this land was still so much a riddle. She knew so little—how it was created, how best controlled—not even the most skilled adepts seemed able to explain its workings to her. The connection to the web of power was a mystery held close by those in the Matriarch's bloodline. And now, with the Matriarch gone...

Devira shifted in her chair, leaned closer and lowered her voice. "Do not fear, young Matriarch. My sister has sworn to keep the secret of the stone. Not difficult, seeing as we know so little about it. Other than its use as a tool to destroy our realm's greatest protection." The Physica leaned back in her chair. "She may no longer hold any sisterly affection for me, but she does not hold much love for the politics and machinations of the Council. She can be trusted in this, I assure you."

Kira nodded, recalling her encounters with Devira's twin. The woman held an anger toward her that Kira was unable to account for. Yet, Aertine had been the one to activate the memory pendant that had caused Kira to recall who she was after her memories had been lost in the strange mist that had separated her from Milos when they first journeyed to this land. Had it been only a few short moons ago? It seemed as if a lifetime had passed.

She reached up and traced her fingers over the raised design in the medallion. The pendant had held so much more, including the memories passed on to her from her mother. She leaned back in her chair and shook her head. In a sense it truly had been a lifetime ago. With the unraveling of recent events, her own destiny had taken a rapid turn and she was no longer the same. No longer the young woman who had come to this land seeking knowledge of her origins. Now, though, she wished her questions had been left unanswered, that she had never discovered the truth. That she had stayed in Tem Hold with Milos.

She pushed the selfish notion aside. These people, her people—if not by upbringing, by blood—needed her. Had she not come, who knows what might have become of them? Kavyn's hands were stained with more blood and sorrow than the demise of his mother, the Matriarch. Who knows where his treachery might have ended? "Do you think she can tell anything from the shards that were left behind when the stone shattered?" Kira sank down in her chair as the weighted memory of that day rekindled her anger and sorrow. If not for Kavyn—and the machinations of his dead mentor Teraxin—things would be much different than they were now. Kira might not be trapped here, searching for a way to revive the powers of this island country.

She thought again of Milos, of the ship that would soon take him far from her and bit back the blaming thoughts. She reminded herself that it had been her own choices that had led her here. From the moment when, at sixteen, she had disregarded Heresta's warnings and ran off with Toril, she had taken her destiny into her own hands. Her subsequent suffering, though not her fault, had been a result of that choice. And, if she had not chosen to escape from Toril, she never would have met Milos. And that was something she could never regret.

Devira cleared her throat, bringing Kira back from her thoughts. "You believe she will find an answer to the mystery of the stone?" she asked the Physica.

"Truly?" Devira's face took on a thoughtful expression. "She is the only one among our people with the talent to do so. If she cannot parse the secret of the stone from its remainders, then I fear that secret will forever lie hidden inside the remains of your brother's broken mind."

She said it so casually, Kira could only wonder how the woman managed not to be roused to ire each time she spoke of the man who had tried to kill her. It was some time before the Physics were able to confirm Devira would live, even longer before they could be certain she would not remain permanently bedridden from the fall down the Guardian's stair. She had lived, not because Kavyn had not intended to kill her, but because he had not cared enough to be thorough, and because all the best Physics in the House of Healing had given their strength and expertise to save her. Yet, she did not seem to hold enmity with him. Perhaps, because his own punishment had been much worse than what he had inflicted.

Kira couldn't imagine that hurt on top of what Devira had already suffered at the hands of the Matriarch. Nor could she fathom the ability to be so forgiving of it.

She let go of the medallion and stared down at the rug that blanketed the floor, tracing the threads of the carpet's pattern with her eyes, trying not to think about Kavyn's vacant stare, the way his eyes looked but did not see. Was he trapped behind those empty orbs? Or had he vanished completely, leaving behind an empty container that only looked like her brother.

Half brother, she reminded herself. They shared only the blood of their father, who had been the Matriarch's consort, not that of the Matriarch herself. Kira still found herself wondering if, like her mother Ardea, she could have given away her only babe in order to try and save a royal line. It seemed too big a sacrifice to even consider. Then again, how could the Matriarch have been willing to see beyond her consort's affair with her son's nursemaid, and her closest friend, to make such a request? Was there more to it than two women acting only in the best interests of their land and people?

Devira shifted in her seat and inclined her head toward the still-shuttered window. "The sun will be up soon. I must go and oversee the day's healing. In addition to the day-to-day ailments, there seems to be no end to the many ways that people manage to harm themselves, and even one another. Especially now, with so many of our people training in hand-to-hand combat." With a sigh, she pushed herself up, moving in a slow, measured manner. Weariness combined with a lack of energy from her recent hurts, Kira

11

thought, gazing at the Physica. That and heartache. She well knew how the woman must feel on that score.

Though the Physica's age, must also contribute. Kira hadn't noticed before, but now she saw the years that had begun to creep in at the edges of the woman's face.

"I would be happy to lend my hands to help with the healing. Though my skills are mainly those linked to herbal knowledge and basic wound tending." Kira stood, a momentary dizziness sweeping over her and she reached out to steady herself, her hand gripping the back of her chair.

Devira's eyes narrowed and she moved closer to Kira. "Is something wrong?"

"No." Kira let go of the chair. "I merely rose too quickly. It is still early and I have not yet broken my fast." She gestured to the faint light that had just begun to seep in through the shutters.

Devira glanced toward the window and cocked her head to one side, giving Kira a quizzical look. Then the older woman's face schooled itself into a healer's blank slate, and she waved a hand at Kira. "I think you have enough responsibilities at the moment, without taking on those of another." She stopped and turned back when she reached the door. "The Council..."

"Will have to be satisfied with the answer I have already given them." Kira wrapped her arms around herself, thankful that the moment of dizziness had passed. She had merely risen too quickly. That was all.

"As you say." Devira bowed her head in acquiescence. "But I expect you will have a more formal visit before long." She closed the door quietly behind her.

After the Physica's departure, Kira paced the room, her agitation growing as the morning sky lightened outside her window. The Gilded Hawk would be preparing to depart. She crossed the room and flung open the shutters, allowing the red-gold of the early morning sun to penetrate into the room. Simply a new dawning for so many others, the rising sun mocked her with its inevitability. What might she give to spend one more day, one more night, with Milos? But there was no holding back time.

Vaith flew across the room, landing on the wide fireplace mantle, and hopped from one foot to the other, making a chittering sound and flapping his wings impatiently.

"When are you not hungry?" Kira glared at him. His wings drooped and her heart softened. She stepped close and stroked his head with her fingertips. "I'm sorry, Little One. I'm out of sorts this morning. Give me a moment to dress and we shall go down to the kitchen and find you a nice tidbit."

Kelmir rumbled his approval.

Chapter 2

Milos slipped his arms inside the fresh shirt and pulled it on. Why he should worry about his appearance, he didn't know. But he dressed and groomed as if preparing for a Hold fete. If he was being honest with himself, he supposed a part of him hoped against hope that Kira might seek him out this day. That she might try to stop him from boarding the Gilded Hawk, beg him not to leave.

The thought of sailing home tore at his heart almost as much as the thought of leaving Kira behind on Eilar. He wondered again if there was anything he might have said or done to change her mind and convince her to go with him. But her answer had been firm. Her words leaving no doubt that her decision was final. She intended to stay here and rule this land. A land she should have looked upon as one filled with strangers. He chastised himself for his resentful thinking. This was also the land of her kin. And who knew what strange blood bond might have been invoked upon her setting foot here. There were so many things about this land and its people that he couldn't begin to understand. And the way the mists had toyed with his mind made him wonder once more if her memories had returned to her intact. Perhaps, he mused, her recollections of their time together had been obscured by that fog, and the right words might reawaken her feelings...

He shook off the moment of wishful thinking and shoved his feet into his worn leather boots. Marquon had offered to have a new pair made for him, but Milos had refused. It seemed somehow fitting to him that the footwear that had borne him here should also return him home, no matter how mean and beggarly it had become. Besides, his rough boots suited his equally rough mood.

The sun would be up soon, the ship preparing to leave, and he wanted at the very least to say farewell to Zharik before departing. The stallion had been with him for so long, he felt he was leaving behind a part of himself by stabling the horse here until the next season's sea trade. The idea chafed at him. There was already too much of him staying behind in Eilar. But the Gilded Hawk was a small sloop built for speed, with a shallower draft than most trade vessels. It had no room for large livestock and would already be over-weighted and crowded taking on the Aestrons in addition to its own crew and the standard shipment of Eilaran goods. And there was no more time to spare. The sea trading season had already neared its end, and the Gilded Hawk was the last ship setting out from Eilar and had already delayed as long as it might to accommodate the stranded Aestrons.

He slipped on his leather jerkin and strapped on his sword before gazing one last time around the cozy room Marquon had assigned him during his time as the Eilaran Protectorate Training Master. A part of him wished the Captain of the Gilded Hawk had refused the delay, that he and the Sunfleet's stranded crew might be forced to stay through until the next season, but he knew also that would only have stretched out his misery. No, he needed to get on with his life and, he admitted, a part of him longed for home.

He had dreamed of travel as a Holder's younger son, hoping for grand adventure and plenty of tales to tell in his dotage, but he had never expected this. Never expected to find himself in a land as strange as Eilar and coming to care for the people almost as much as he did those of his own Holding. "It's no longer yours," he reminded himself as he hoisted the pack with his few belongings onto his shoulder. "You let go of it when you left." But, he realized, he hadn't really let go of Tem Hold and its people. They were still in his heart and would remain there, right beside the memory of his long-departed brother.

And now his feelings for Kira.

The stables were dark when he arrived, silent except for Zharik's low whicker of recognition as Milos entered the barn. "Hello, old friend," Milos murmured when Zharik leaned his head over the stall door and huffed out his warm breath. Milos stroked the horse's forehead and scratched behind his left ear.

Zharik pushed forward and tilted his head to bring himself eye-to-eye with Milos, as if the horse were attempting to read his thoughts. Milos's chest tightened. "I'd give most anything to be able to share my mind with you as Kira does with her companions," he said. "Though I fear it would only make this parting more difficult. Marquon will bring you home on the first ship of the next trade season. Though, that will be some moons from now." He patted Zharik's neck.

"You'll be in good hands, till then." He held out the green apple he'd brought with him and Zharik gripped it between his teeth and snapped it in half, spraying pulp and juice up Milos's sleeve. "Well, I'll at least have something to remember you by for the first part of my voyage," he said, in an attempt to make himself feel lighter as he brushed the bits of fruit from his shirt. But the sense of impending loss only weighed heavier on him as he strode out of the stables and headed for the docks and the ship that waited to take him back to Aestron.

Chapter 3

The House of Learning hummed with energy and the murmur of Masters as they guided their students.

Kira sat upon a woven mat that covered the floor, attempting to ignore the buzzing energy that poured from the students in the surrounding rooms. When first she'd started these lessons, she thought she could readily accept her status as a beginner. But day after day, as she passed by the other students, most of whom were many years her junior, her frustration grew as she struggled to grasp the threads of each lesson. She had begun to wonder if her sense of self might become as fragile as a hen's egg.

"Stop thinking," Master Amark chided, as if he could sense her wandering mind. "Remember, you must relax your shields and concentrate your thoughts upon a single focal point."

Kira grunted with the effort, but still she could not find her way in.

"It's not a hammer," she heard the Master repeat over and over, his words coming to her as though in a dream. "Ease up."

She sensed a nudge of energy on the back of her neck and loosened her grip on the power, letting her barriers drop enough to allow the teacher's mind to guide her. It was akin to having another person place their hand over hers on a sword's pommel and help guide the motion of the blade through the air, only it was much more difficult not to fight against another's mental energies. It gave her an odd sensation like trying to float on her back in water that was too shallow.

"Now, feel your way along the surface. Find the spirit of the stone, the root of its creation, the beginning of its energy. Meld your mind with it. Reach for it as you would one of your companions."

Kira tried to do as he said, but the idea of connecting mentally with a stone was on the one hand incomprehensible and on the other ludicrous. And there was also something frightening about it.

She pushed against the surface, nudging it, felt it begin to stretch, then winced as it snapped back into a solid, unforgiving surface.

Beside her, Master Amark sat silent. He took in a deep breath, then let it out once more. "Again," he said, his voice neutral but firm. "Try again."

Chapter 4

Aertine cleared her workspace and set the shards before her. This time, she placed the bits and pieces in a semi-circular pattern, using the length of silver wire to link them together. She held her hand above the fragments of stone and closed her eyes. Once more the odd sensations rose up from the broken bits, weaving themselves into a ribbon of energy that swelled and broke apart again before she could come close to connecting with it.

She pulled her hand away and eyed the chips of stone warily. There was something she was missing. Something that kept her from discerning the energies that had been impressed upon the stone. Just as it had when she'd struggled to connect the memories of her family's keep.

A scuff outside the workroom pulled her attention to the doorstep.

"Good morn," Varnon said as he entered, setting down a worn wicker hamper on the small table just inside the door.

Aertine sent a sour glance through the doorway at the brightening sky. "Is it?"

"You've not been up all night again?" He shook his head

as he rolled up his shirtsleeves, preparing for the day's work.

Aertine wiped at her eyes. "I'm missing something," she said in frustration.

"Sleep is what you are missing, Mistra Aertine, if I may be so bold."

"You may not," she scolded. "I am still the skilled master—"

"And I, the lowly apprentice, should know my place?" he chided.

"The promise of pairing clearly agrees with you." Aertine gathered up the pieces of polished stone and placed them back into the leather pouch that hung at her waist. "You never spoke with such confidence before Dravyne said yes."

"Indeed. Though, if not for my sister's impending pairing, I doubt I would have been emboldened enough to ask."

"Your parents' household empties, yet grows. They must be pleased to add to the family's branching."

"They are. Though, our mother can hardly focus herself on a single aspect of Viel's upcoming pairing celebration without worrying how it will compare to Dravyne's mother's preparations."

Aertine paused for a moment in deep thought. "Perhaps, they should combine their efforts," she murmured more to herself than to Varnon.

"Perhaps." He gave her a quizzical look. "Since you have not slept, I would venture to assume you have also not eaten."

She waved him off. "I'm fine."

"Just as well, then." Smiling, he lifted up the basket he'd brought with him and set it before her. "As a matter of course, my lovely promised sends her regards. And a loaf of her best." He raised the lid of the basket. "I cannot say I will regret having to eat it alone."

The aroma of fresh-baked bread wafted up and Aertine's mouth watered as she peeked inside the basket. "Is that a portion of her honey and lavender cheese?"

"It is."

"I might well be persuaded to break my fast on this." Aertine reached into the basket, then pulled out the clay dish. She removed the lid, raised the container up to her face and inhaled. "Mmmmm. No one makes a cheese as good."

"I'll tell her you said so. Again." Varnon laughed as he emptied the rest of the basket's contents onto the table.

Aertine opened another container. "Lissom berry jam?" she blurted in surprise.

He grinned.

"This early in the year, it must be the last of her past season set aside."

"The very last. She insisted I share it with you. I tried to tell her you wouldn't accept, but what could I do?" He forced a frown and placed a hand over his heart. "I suffer so on your behalf." His merry eyes betrayed his words.

"You made a fine choice when you asked her." Aertine dipped a spoon into the jam and smeared it on a bit of bread already slathered in the rich cheese.

"I am well aware of that, Mistra. Though, truth be known, as it turns, she was set to ask me had I not made the effort. I am a lucky man indeed." He set the basket off to the side and sat down at the table. He scooped jam onto a hunk of bread. "Now, tell me what it is you are working on that sets your jaw on edge so."

"A special project," she said between bites. "The details of which I am unable to share at this time."

His face fell.

"Don't look so forlorn," Aertine chided. "It has nothing to do with the level of your skills."

And everything to do with mine, she thought.

Chapter 5

Ekzarn placed his hand upon the glowing crystal and sank deep, connecting with the faint power lines that ebbed and flowed far below him beneath the sea. He pulled himself along one line and then another, until he was able to grasp the frazzled edges of the deeper flows of energy that crisscrossed the Island of Eilar.

It took every ounce of strength to pull himself up the jagged broken line. Though the force of the line filled him with an exultant surge, he knew his body would rebel again once he returned to it, that it would betray him with its frailty, and the longer he touched the power, the greater would be the price once he let go of it. No matter. He must push forward, must reach the gap.

Once there, he edged his way along the brittle fracture, searching, testing. There must be a thread, a spark, some way to bridge the abyss that yawned before him and kept him at bay.

But, as usual, he was unable to leap the breach and gain the thread that would allow him access to the Guardian's seat.

And the root of Eilar's power.

He'd been so close when Kavyn had let him in. But Matriarch Kyrina had continued to hold him at bay. Day in and day out, he had battered at her shields. And, finally, her barriers had begun to yield. But even with the upstart Kavyn's added efforts, Ekzarn had been unable to destroy the damned woman's defenses.

And with the destruction of the focusing stone, he had been shoved out, once more denied his due.

This fresh banishment was so complete, it felt like being exiled all over again. The mere thought of the buffeting energy of the Council's mindwalls as they slammed into place against him, renewed his hatred.

It fueled his rage. How dare those people, his own people, ban him from his homeland and the gateway to the source of power. How dare they send him out into an empty world devoid of the thoughts of others. The casting out had rendered him deaf and blind. The sudden silence had nearly destroyed him. He'd been utterly alone when his small boat had washed ashore upon the Outer Isles. The old fisherwoman who'd found him and taken him in, had muttered to him under her breath as she dragged him from the boat and laid him out upon the sand beside her tiny shack, but he'd been unable to understand her. He'd swum in a haze of darkness as she'd tended to him, treating him like a lost pet.

Yes, she'd been crazy, her mind having flown before he had arrived, but that hadn't mattered. Not then. Not until the day... Perhaps, if she'd been sane. If he had not been so outside of himself, he might have been able to control his rage. But, no. She'd brought her ending upon herself. He tore his mind away, hastily reinterred the memory of those days. He needed to focus. The edge was too near, too jagged a power. He could not afford to be distracted.

In the end, it would all belong to him. He would own Eilar and everything that lay above and below it. He would tap the line and drink from it, guzzle it, make it his. And once that power was his to control, he would end them all.

He let his mental energies expand, allowing his mind to relax and roam, seeking an open path across the severed connection, or another twisted mind like Kavyn's had been before becoming the drooling wreck he was since the destruction of the focus stone. He searched for any opening that might allow him egress, but try as he might, he could not cross the barrier.

The denial of access was like a burning poker that stabbed into his heart. *I will have Eilar,* he thought, as his energies seeped back into him. He let the pain of his broken body fuel his ire. *The Guardian's seat belongs to me. And I will destroy anything and anyone that stands in my way.*

It would be the fleet that would take the land. His raiders would bring him home, but first he needed to know everything about the enemy he would face once there. He needed to parse the strength of the Matriarch's heir. The one who had stood up to Kavyn and destroyed their well-laid plans. The one who had returned and denied him his right. The one who had chosen to stand in his way and now must fall before his might.

Chapter 6

Milos tossed his belongings onto the hammock nearest Dahl's. He would have preferred to be nearer the hatch, but the boy had already been assigned a spot near the bulkhead. They'd come this far together, and Milos wasn't about to abandon the boy now.

He glanced around the tight quarters, watching the remaining members of the Sunfleet ship's crew settle in for the voyage home.

The men had remained less than friendly toward him, and the boy had been treated roughly due to his friendship.

Milos let out a growl of frustration. Once more he wondered if he was doing the right thing. True, the boy needed his protection, but only because of their close association over time. Would not the ship's crew welcome him back into their fold if Milos had distanced himself? But how could he? Dahl had always looked to the Sunfleet's Captain as a father figure, and now Captain Salker was gone. Milos felt he owed the boy.

He glanced over at the Sunfleet's First Mate Stronar, who eyed him with contempt. Perhaps distancing himself wouldn't help. The ship's mate held to a grudge the way a starving dog holds onto a bone. And there was truly nothing to keep Milos on Eilar. Kira had shown her true leanings once she had found her way back home.

The Matriarch. Of all things. He shook his head in wonder, still unable to accept it all. And her offer to him? The position of Consort? He had given up all his worldly ties to be with her, and there she was, offering him scraps from the Eilaran high table.

He immediately chastised himself for the thought.

"Milos?" Dahl jumped down the ship's ladder and grabbed him by the sleeve. "Did you see the messenger?"

"Messenger?"

"A messenger has come aboard, asking for you."

Milos' heart jumped. Could it be a message from Kira? Might she have changed her mind? "Where, Dahl? Where is this messenger?"

"Above decks." The boy pointed.

Milos wasted no time. He grabbed the rails of the ladder and flew up and out of the hatch. On deck, he glanced around, searching for the messenger, and started when he saw his friend, Marquon.

The man strode across the deck, his boot heels clapping against the wood. "There you are," he called as he closed the distance between them.

Milos frowned. "Are you running messages now?"

"No, no. It was the only way they'd let me on board so close to cast off," he said in a low voice. He stepped back a pace and held out his hand in greeting.

Milos responded in kind. "Then, to what do I owe the pleasure of this visit?"

"I merely wanted the opportunity to try once more..."

"I thank you for all you and your people have done," Milos said. "But I have not changed my mind. My course is set." He gazed ashore, his eyes drawn to the Keep that towered above the rest of the settlement. "I belong in

Aestron with my own people."

"So be it, my friend. But I do have a parting gift for you," the big man said, extending his hand. In it lay a gleaming crystal, faceted and polished. It glittered in the early sunlight.

Milos eyed the stone warily. "It won't grab me as the sentry stone did?"

Marquon laughed. "No."

Milos took the stone from him and held it up to the light, admiring the colors it reflected in the sunlight. "What does it do?"

"It's merely a keepsake. Sadly, an aged and dying one. An illumin-crystal, which once held light." He clapped Milos on the shoulder. "A small bit of Eilar to take with you on your journey."

"Thank you," Milos said. "I will miss our conversations, and our verbal repartee, but not your riddles."

"Nor our actual parrying?"

"Indeed," Milos said, his tone good-natured. He flexed his sword arm and rotated his shoulder, causing his friend to laugh.

Marquon took his leave and Milos stepped to the ship's railing to watch his friend depart. Marquon strode down the gangplank, turning when he reached the dock to place his left hand over his heart and give Milos a quick nod before continuing on his way.

Milos returned the gesture. One that held more meaning than the many words the two men had left unspoken.

A shadow slipped up beside him, becoming Dahl. "You'd rather stay, wouldn't you?"

Milos said nothing. The boy could read his heart and there was no need to answer.

"But..." Dahl's face grew fearful.

"But, what?" Milos asked. "What worries you?"

"You're still coming with us. Going home, to Aestron. Aren't you?" He shifted his feet and braced himself against the rail, as if expecting a rolling wave to rock the ship. "You'll return...with...us?"

Milos nodded.

He turned and gazed out across the expanse of water that lay between him and Aestron. Between him and Tem Hold. The barrier that would soon lie between him and his heart's desire.

"So be it." His murmured words were too quiet for the boy to hear, but Dahl's face had already relaxed in the knowledge that he would not be left alone to fend for himself aboard a ship of men who were no longer friends.

"I will return," Milos said, "to where I am needed most."

Chapter 7

Devira cupped her aching hands to her chest, allowing the warmth of her body to seep into her cold crooked fingers, then leaned her head back against the padded headrest, meditating on the swirling patterns of the Physic's chamber wall before her. The surrounding crystals glowed faintly, casting luminescent streaks across the carved designs. Shadows slid into the recesses, seeming to shift and coil in on themselves as she sank deeper into the healing sea of mental energies. She let her gnarled hands slip down into her lap as the ebb and flow of energy calmed her, dulling her constant pain.

Deeper and deeper she descended into the space between waking and sleep, midway between dark and light, to the inmost place of healing.

"Devira." Her whispered name floated to her deep in the void.

"Devira." Someone calling to her from far off.

"Zoshia?" she murmured, not wanting to leave the dreamy state where her hands were no longer painful anchors that held her tied to the waking shore, but feeling the drag of consciousness tugging her back. "Zoshia?" She sat up, startled into full waking.

Her lifemate knelt before her, dark hollows beneath her eyes making her face appear thin and frail. "Hello, my love. I've missed you."

Devira reached out a hand, brushing Zoshia's face with the back of her scarred fingers. "You're really here?"

"I am." Zoshia gently placed her palm against Devira's.

"I've missed you, too." Devira's eyes welled and she used her sleeve to wipe the tears away before they could drift down her cheeks.

"Then, you've forgiven me?" Zoshia asked, the question making her appear vulnerable in a way Devira had never before known the Council Second to be.

"Our differences seem much less...important, now."

Zoshia leaned forward and placed her forehead against Devira's. Though Devira knew better than to allow her mind to push outward, the physical gesture of trust and love warmed her. "I hate when we fight," she said.

Zoshia laughed lightly and pulled away just far enough to peer into her lifemate's eyes. "We've never fought like *that* before." Her eyes glittered in the half-light.

"That does nothing to change the fact that I hated it." Devira felt her own eyes working to fill themselves with unshed tears.

"As did I," Zoshia said, sitting on her heels and staring up her. "Let us never do so again."

Devira slid from the seat to the floor and rested her head upon Zoshia's shoulder. "Would that I could promise you that," she said, her tears finally slipping free.

Zoshia wrapped an arm around her and hugged her close. "Let us both attempt it, then." She kissed Devira, warm and sweet.

Feeling herself floating in the warmth of their love and desires, Devira's thoughts turned. Better this than all the healing meditations in the land, she thought. She wrapped her arms around her beloved. But what will she say when I tell her of our work with the shattered stone? She pushed away the worry to save for another day. For this moment, here and now, she would allow herself some small shard of happiness.

Chapter 8

"Marquon," Tesalin called out to him as he entered the open compound, her voice raised to be heard above the clacking and clanging of weapons and shields. "You're alone." Her words held an accusatory tone as she crossed the grounds to meet him.

"He refused me, as you anticipated."

"You owe me five cooling crystals, then." Tesalin held out her hand with a smirk of satisfaction, though her smile did not reach her eyes.

Marquon eyed her empty palm a moment, then shook his head. "It isn't as if I carry them around in my pouch."

"Perhaps, you should, if you plan to make a habit of betting on losing gambles." She shrugged. "No matter. I know where to find you." She left him standing in the compound's entryway.

Before him, the protectorate's men and women practiced what Milos had taught them, sharing the knowledge through means both mental and physical. No longer were the militia's members forced to hide themselves, they now had Council approval to recruit and train as many Eilaran as were willing. A need they had finally admitted to with the fall of the island's defenses.

Marquon wondered at the Protectorate's swelling numbers. Apparently, he was not alone in his need to do something to protect their land. Many people shared a concern for the safety of families and friends. Especially those with weaker gifts. They seemed to feel the need to do something, anything, to help.

All were certain that it was a mere matter of time before the Outland raiders came at them again seeking to destroy their island. Though none knew why. Theirs was not a land of wealth, not in the sense that interested most people. Yet, the Outlanders had tested them. Had sent those small groups of ships at their shore. He knew in his heart that attack had only been the first volley. When the storm of war surged, it would try and wash over their shores. They must be prepared for the fury of it when it came.

Marquon wondered once more why only the normally protected shores had been tested, those places where the Net alone had been incorporated, and not the island's shipping ports, where the physical barriers and protections from sea attacks could be moved into place. In fact, the Outlanders had attacked strategically, targeting only those places where the island's protective Net had been torn asunder.

How had they known?

"Marquon," a young voice called. "Will you show the new recruits the moves you've been developing?"

He rolled his shoulders and flexed his arms to limber himself and strode across the grounds, catching a staff that was tossed in his direction as he passed. These newest trainees could use the challenge, and the distraction would do him good. He spun the staff over his head and brought it down in front of him, falling into a defensive stance and issuing a challenge to the nearest recruit.

Chapter 9

Kira entered the room with tentative steps. Kavyn sat propped in the bed, head bent forward. His eyes were closed, dried spittle glinting from the corner of his mouth.

"Kavyn?" she asked, wondering if he could even hear her. He slid open his eyes and rolled his head as if attempting to focus. After a moment, he grunted and let his head fall back onto his chest.

She pulled up a chair beside the bed and leaned forward. "Kavyn, I need to speak with you." The mentalists told her there was still some sense of him inside, though they were unsure how much, if anything, he might understand. But she had to try. Needed to understand what he had planned. Needed to discover the key to unlock the shattered stone's purpose.

His eyes remained closed, but his face twitched. Was it involuntary, as some of the Physics believed? Or was he there, behind the visage? She leaned closer, seeking a glimmer of thought within the shell that lay before her, but there was nothing, no sign that he could even hear her.

The mentalists had warned her. His mind was not only

broken, his barriers were, as well. Closing him off. Closing him in. The mentalists had been unable to reach him through normal methods and extremes were unthinkable. None would dare to break their oath to do so. But her options were dwindling, and she'd hoped they were wrong, that she'd be able to reach him, to ask him of the stone; how it was made; what it could be used for; whether or not it could be mended.

Though, if she were being honest with herself, she knew the question she'd really wanted answered was why. True, he'd been placed in a secondary role by birth. She understood what it meant to fight against tradition, to be different. But his ambition and poor choices had only led him here.

Locked inside himself.

Kira couldn't imagine the grief of losing her connection with Vaith or Kel. She shuddered to think what it would be like to be trapped within the walls of one's own mind, unable to lift the barriers, to communicate at all with those outside one's self.

She reached out and touched a tentative finger to his wrist and some of the anger she held against him melted away. Startled, she pulled back. What was she thinking, feeling sorry for him? He'd plotted with assassins, destroyed the protections of an entire people. He'd killed his own mother, for Troka's sake!

She stepped away from the sickbed, eyeing him warily. Wanting him to outwardly be the monster she knew lurked inside. But he looked like a broken doll, and her healer's instincts pushed her to care. And she hated feeling that way about him. She had a sudden urge to slap him, to pound her fists into him, to pick up the poker from the hearth...

She stormed back to the bed, raised her fist, then froze, frightened by the strength of the rage that had washed over her, relieved that no one else had been there to witness it.

She backed away from his still form and sank down into the window seat and gazed out at the white clouds that scudded across the sky, letting the anger seep out of her. Why had she even come here? Even if he could speak, she thought, there was no reason he would tell her anything. The afternoon breeze pushed the clouds past the window and carried in the smell of late summer blossoms: penstemon, dapple flowers and sunspurs. The familiar scents calmed her pounding blood. She closed her eyes and leaned her head upon the sill.

Chapter 10

Ekzarn fumed. Things had truly taken a sharp turn since he'd laid his plans for vengeance, so many years ago. True, he had ensured the death of the Matriarch Kyrina's consort. That had been a bit of beautiful maneuvering on his part. Planting such seeds from so far a distance had taken no less than every ounce of strategizing he could bring to bear. Not to mention the ongoing manipulation of those weak-minded puppets, Teraxin and his accomplices. No mean feat for an exile who had been driven to the far corner of an inhospitable land filled with backward, barbaric people.

If the Outlanders were more astute, they might realize what minor pawns they really were. But Ekzarn had played them well and surely. Continued to do so. He pushed himself up out of his high-backed chair, gripping the arms of his seat to steady himself. All of his work had taken a heavy toll. Using the locus stone had been exhausting, both physically and mentally. His withered muscles and bowed back were proof enough of that. Though, his suffering would be worth every ounce of energy he had expended, every fiber and sinew that had weakened and betrayed him, once he sat upon the Guardian's Seat. He would sink into the energy stream, bathe in it, and heal himself. Nay, he would do more, he would remake his body into an impenetrable fortress.

He rolled his head to ease the tension in his neck and shoulders, then gripped the thick staff he carried and used it as a cane to drag his weakened body across the room.

Had Kavyn been less of a fool, Ekzarn would already be in possession of the Eilaran Island and all its treasures. But the sniveling pup had been too full of himself, too convinced of his own destiny to break the matriarchal chain. Teraxin had played that hand a little too well. And what did he have to show for it? Dead at the hands of a tool of his own forging. Fitting.

Though, how could they have accounted for the return of the Matriarch's heir? She should have been dead, drowned in the stinking sea, along with her idiot wet-nurse. Or destroyed when Ekzarn's Outlanders had raided that stinking pit they'd escaped to. Well, now the line would be severed completely and with certainty. No more wandering relatives to cause a ripple in his plans. The Guardian's throne would finally be his. And once installed upon that great seat, he would make his enemies pay.

His thoughts drifted back to that fateful day, when he had made his thoughts known to the Matriarch. At first, he had sought only to be an equal to her, to sit beside her on the Guardian's throne, to share in the power of position. But she had made excuses, claiming the seat had only room for one ruler—that the land could not abide with two. And when he had shown her what he had discovered of his own volition, the ways to which he could put his gifts to work, proof that he was beyond them all...she had blanched and dismissed him, telling him she must think on things.

He'd gone to his quarters, confident in his claim to

power, never suspecting they would come for him as he slept, that they would treat him as a common criminal, would block him from the source, deny him his due...

No. He refused to revisit his trial at the hands of the interrogators. He had done no more nor less than he had a right to do. They should have elevated him. She *should* have celebrated his display of skill, his abilities to do what no other had dared, to use the power of the land to become more than a mere Guardian. Instead, she had run to the Council.

And the Council had ruined him.

They dredged up ancient laws prohibiting the turning of the land's power to the service of those who were most capable. Laws that had surely been devised simply to keep an adept of his ilk from fulfilling his destiny. They had used those laws to exile him, ripping him from the land, tearing him from his birthright.

And, as a final insult, the Matriarch had elevated that weak upstart Verun as her consort, claiming that his humility would best serve the people of Eilar.

Ekzarn pounded his staff upon the floor in his frustration. Humility! He would show them what it meant to be humbled.

His chest heaved and he sucked in a lungful of air and then another, reaching for the draft of medicinal herbs that was always nearby. He gulped down one swallow of the bitter dregs and then another. Finally, he downed the last of the potion and shuddered at the loosening of his chest as his breathing returned to normal.

Once upon the Guardian's Seat, he promised himself, this frailty that had taken him would be relieved. No matter the cost. He would be whole. He would drag the Eilaran from the past and into a new day.

And the Matriarch's line would be severed. Forever.

Chapter 11

Kira wiped her face with the cooling towel. The sickness had come over her so sudden, she'd almost had no time to reach her own room and the chamber pot within. Was this sickness a remnant of the change that had been forced upon her in the Guardian's chamber? Had the Matriarch imparted more than what Kira knew? Or was there some sickness of the land that she should be aware of? Something related to the deaths of so many of the young gifted? She thought of the children she passed each day in the House of Learning.

She closed her eyes and, bit by bit, let down the barriers that walled her from the powerful connection to the land, allowing herself to be pulled into the flow of power. As she opened herself to the land, the sickness abated, her senses came alive and her entire body buzzed with the energy that flowed through the realm. The lines, as she explored them, became broken and jagged near the guardian stones, those places where her brother Kavyn had damaged the flow and destroyed the protections that had been put in place to protect their island. Incredible that the small stone he'd used had held such destructive power.

She inched her way outward, slowly letting in more and more of the land's power. Her body felt light, as if she could float on the air. Her senses reached out, seeking the ends of the land, the places where the lines dove into the sea. She had never allowed herself to venture beyond the shore. Would the lines end? Did she only have the power to connect with and sense the land as far as the Eilaran realm went? Or might she reach beyond those boundaries?

Tentatively, she let herself slip farther and farther away, letting the rolling sea wash over her. Her body relaxed, basking in the cool deep water, where the sun's rays barely rippled overhead. Deeper and deeper she slid until darkness and depth were all she knew.

Suddenly, a hand reached out, grasping her and dragging her farther from the shore. Deeper and deeper, until the pressure of the ocean crushed her chest, forcing the breath from her lungs.

Gasping for air, she flung her barriers back up and tumbled over and over, slamming back into her body with a painful crash. She lay there shuddering with a cold that seemed to have wedged itself deep inside her.

The echo of a frustrated growl rang out in her mind. Something or someone filled with malice had wanted to crush her and was furious at the loss of its prey.

Chapter 12

The ship rocked, rolling over the heavy waves. As much as Milos wanted to believe the Captain's skills would keep them safe, he couldn't shake the memory of the storm in which he'd nearly lost everything. Then again, he thought wryly of the uncertainties of life, it seemed he truly had. It was true, Marquon planned to bring Zharik back to Aestron for him, but that was moons away and, as recent events had shown, a great deal could change in a short amount of time.

His gaze rose up to the top of the mast where he knew Dahl was stationed keeping a watch on the horizon. At least, the boy had survived their voyage and would be home with his family soon.

It pained Milos to feel like a passenger on this voyage, while the rest of the crew worked their passage for the crossing. But the captain had insisted his fare had been paid. Milos had no idea who his benefactor might be, though he suspected it must be Marquon. He had attempted to turn back the captain's offer, but the man would have none of it.

"Your bold actions have not gone unnoticed," the Captain had told him. "Nor is it a secret that you helped to drill our militia. Without them, and your valiant efforts, our island would have been overrun by the raiders and would now be even more defenseless than it is." With that, the captain had ushered him aside, in order to bellow orders at the men bringing aboard and stowing the cargo intended for Aestron.

Trade would need to increase in order to support the island with the tools and weapons necessary to defend itself from the Outland raiders should they decide to come at them again.

"Heyo," a voice called.

Milos looked up in time to see Dahl shinny down the rope ladder and swing to the deck. "Your injury has healed well," Milos said as the boy skittered across the planking to stand beside him.

"Aye," the boy rubbed at his arm. "Those healers know their work."

"Physics," Milos reminded him, his thoughts flying back to Eilar. "Their people call them Physics."

Dahl shrugged. "Not sure why the name matters. They healed the whole crew up well and good." He glanced around and lowered his voice. "Not that it done a bit to change the first mate's gripes." His face dropped into a frown. "Nor did they have the magic to bring back our Captain." His lower lip quivered only the slightest bit before he tightened his jaw.

"Saving a life is much more difficult than taking one," Milos told him. "And I've not heard of any healer, specially skilled or otherwise, who can give life back to those who have rejoined the wheel. Your captain was a good man. Trust that Troka will be kind."

"I know," Dahl whispered. "But I don't understand why it is that someone as good as the captain had to die and—"

"And some other lesser man might live?" A gruff voice

44

said from behind them.

The boy spun around to see the angry face of the Sunfleet's First Mate, Stronar. Dahl stood his ground. "If the sailcloth fits."

The big man growled and took a step toward the boy, but Milos moved between them. "I understand the Captain of the Hawk does not take kindly to brawling on his ship."

Stronar let loose a sour laugh. "'Don't take a brawl to squash a pestering nit." He spat on the deck just missing the boy's feet.

Dahl started forward, but Milos put a hand on his shoulder. "I thought you were going to show me how to tie those knots."

The boy studied him sharply. "Aye. But not till my watch is over. I've got to go help in the mess till then."

"I'll meet you after." Milos gave his shoulder a squeeze and eyed the mate. "And do me a favor and make sure no one is spitting into the stew, eh?"

"I'll do what I can," Dahl said with a shrug, "but you know how it is in a busy mess. Hard to watch all the cooks all the time." He sneered at the mate as he sauntered toward the galley.

The mate's face turned a darker shade of red. "I were you," he snarled at Milos, "I'd watch who I angered."

"I've earned my share of enemies in my time," Milos told him. "And I've won my share of allies. Perhaps, we should call a truce as long as we are confined to this vessel."

Stronar shook his head and sneered. "You left your allies ashore with that witch. My men and me have no ship, and no Captain, which means we have no pay coming when we land in Aestron, and will all have to seek new berths. It's too late in the season to sign to a crew now, even with the speed of this sloop. So, we arrive home empty-handed. You and your woman are to blame for our losses, but we've received no offer of recompense from either of you, have we? And just because you and that group of island toughs showed up in time to help us fight off those Outlanders, don't make you a hero. It was your fault we were left stranded on that beach at the mercy of what come in the first place. Don't expect us to kiss your boots for that."

"The boy is right," Milos said.

"Right about what?" Stronar sneered.

"Such a waste. For all the Eilaran Physics' healing powers, they couldn't do a thing to change your sour outlook on the world."

Stronar raised his fists, but at that moment the Captain shouted orders. "We'll be settling this later." The big man turned to his duties.

Milos shook his head at his inability to defuse the situation. His own attitude had turned more bitter than he liked to admit. He thought back on the path his life had taken. From Tem Hold's irresponsible younger son to becoming its overly responsible and dour Holder.

And then Kira had stepped into his world.

He stared out at the rolling sea, gazing back to where Eilar lay. If only he had stayed and worked to change her mind. Things might be different. But they were both stubborn. What might she be doing at this moment? He hoped she was thinking of him and missing him as much as he did her.

Chapter 13

Kira paused beneath the branches of yellow blossoms. Reaching up, she plucked one of the last of the season's flowers, savoring the sweet scent that brought with it the memories of her true mother, Ardea, in the time before their frightening flight from their island home. Kelmir, who had been loping ahead, paused in the shade of a broad elderthorn bush and waited. Vaith circled above, bright scales glittering in the sunlight that broke between drifting clouds that floated in the blue expanse overhead. His thoughts pulled at her, tickling her brain and urging her to fly with him.

As much as I would like nothing better than the sense of flying free today, my Princeling, I have other business I must attend to, she sent, wistfully blocking him from her thoughts and giving his mind a gentle nudge.

He squawked in irritation, then turned his back on her in a show of hurt, winging high overhead, soaring away on the eddying air.

Kira rubbed her neck, but did not give in to her companion's pique. Instead, she turned away, forcing her feet to follow the path toward duty and responsibility.

If what Devira said was true, perhaps they could discover the root of Kavyn's focal stone. And if they could replicate it...Kira looked to the sky where Vaith continued to soar freely overhead. Not that it would change things between her and Milos. It was too late for that now. They had made their choices. She opened her fist and let the crumpled flower petals fall to the ground. Yellow pollen stained her palm and she brushed it away as she hurried on.

Kelmir, sensing her determination, trotted ahead in the direction of Aertine's workshop.

Outside the workroom she paused, wondering what sort of welcome she would receive. After the fall of the Matriarch, Aertine had been civil to her, but her politeness clearly did not stem from any warm regard. Though the dual adept had been the one to trigger the return of Kira's memories, she remained distant and cold toward Eilar's new Matriarch.

Kira couldn't blame her. Had the tables been turned, she doubted she'd be inclined to trust the daughter of the woman who had nearly destroyed her sister. If Kira could only tell her who she really was. But that secret was not a thing to be shared. Not with anyone.

Voices lilted from inside the workshop. The rise and fall of conversation broken by a quick laugh.

The sound suddenly irritated her, though she didn't know why it should. Kira squared her shoulders. Well, these people wanted a leader; she would give them one. *Kel, Vaith, to me.*

Kelmir padded up beside her as Vaith swooped to land upon her shoulder. He clutched the leather shoulder pad with stiff talons but refused to wrap his tail about her neck. Obviously, he had still not quite forgiven her. She sighed. Her list of allies appeared to be dwindling. The thought made her scowl. She smoothed her features and took a deep breath, then stepped beneath the shaded overhang and rapped on the door, entering the workshop without waiting.

"Matriarch," a young man gasped, jumping up from his place at the table and holding out both hands in respectful deference, though his eyes strayed nervously to Kelmir as he did so.

Kira stepped forward and held both hands over his in greeting.

Aertine stood and held out a single hand, palm up, in a gesture of welcome but let her hand fall quickly back to her side as Kira reached forward to accept the gesture.

The young man's face registered surprise at the Mistra's less than polite greeting. "Will you break bread with us this fine morning?" he asked nervously, waving to an empty chair and the food arrayed upon the table.

Though her stomach roiled at the thought of food, Kira nodded politely. "Thank you, it was not my intention to intrude."

"Yes, of course," Aertine said, eyes narrowed as she glanced at the door Kira had just barged through. "However, now that you are here, we welcome you to partake in our repast. Dravyne, my apprentice Varnon's young promised, is a fine baker."

"And her cheeses and jams are beyond comparison," the young man said. "Or, so I am told." The grin he flashed Aertine suggested that Kira was missing something. She gave him a quick, polite smile and settled herself into the seat nearest the door.

Vaith shifted from her shoulder to perch upon the back of the chair. His hunger washed over her, causing her stomach to lurch again. "Thank you, I'm not hungry, but I know someone who is." She took a small piece of the fresh bread and tore off a bit to feed to the little wyvern. Kelmir raised his head and sniffed at the bread, but found it decidedly uninteresting and attempted to curl at her feet. However, the three chairs took up most of the space at the

49

table. *Kel, would you be so kind as to sit by the door?*

The big cat rumbled in disapproval, keeping his eyes trained on Aertine and her apprentice as he moved to sit before the door, tensed and alert.

"My apologies for my companion's surliness," she said as she watched him settle. "I've no idea what's bothering him." Though, perhaps she did. It would not be the first time Kelmir had reflected her own tumbling emotions. She sent him an easing thought, but he refused to respond in kind. Surly, indeed. Kira pulled her mind back.

"What brings you to my humble workshop this morn, Matriarch?" Aertine asked, her tone lukewarm.

"I have come to ask of your progress with my...with the stone shards," Kira responded, fighting the urge to flick her eyes at the young man sitting across from her making an effort to seem intent on nothing more than his morning meal.

Aertine tossed the pouch onto the table in frustration. "This is more of a puzzle than attempting to piece together the remainders of my family's defaced memory stone." Her words held a bitter edge. Kira sensed that Aertine's ire had less to do with her frustration at the lack of progress on the task she'd been set, but was instead connected to the animosity the woman held toward her.

The young man busied himself with spreading a soft white cheese onto a piece of bread, his focused intent clearly dedicated to keeping him out of the conversation. And hopefully out of conflict with both his Mistra and his Matriarch, Kira thought.

Vaith rocked from side to side, eyeing the cheese and bread. He let out a squawk when Varnon bit into the food. "Hush, Vaith," Kira scolded.

Varnon tore off a corner of the cheese-covered bread and held it out. "May I?" he asked, a glint of excitement in his eye.

What was it about young men and wyverns? Kira

wondered, hiding the smile that tried to quirk up her mouth. "I apologize for my companion's rudeness," she said, giving Vaith a sideways look of disapproval, "but please do. You will be doing me a kindness to feed him." She raised her wrist over her shoulder, allowing Vaith to step from the back of the chair onto it. Then, she stretched out her arm.

Varnon's eyes opened wide in excitement. "Will he truly allow me to hold him?"

Kira forced herself not to roll her eyes or make fun of the young man's enthusiasm. "He'll be more than happy to stay with you as long as you provide him with food." She gave him a wry smile as he held up his arm for Vaith to step onto.

"He's heavier than I expected." Varnon brought his arm closer to his chest and offered the morsel of food to Vaith.

"He eats enough for two," Kira said, purposely ignoring the twinge of sickness at the thought of so much food.

Beside her, Kelmir rumbled low. "I haven't forgotten you," she chided the big cat. "Do you mind?" she asked Aertine.

Aertine pursed her lips, but at a questioning look from Varnon, she indicated her assent. "Please, Matriarch, do as you will. My home is yours."

Kira ignored the woman's less-than-enthusiastic tone and broke off a bit of the rich cheese, dropping her hand to allow Kelmir to stretch out his neck and lick the crumbling substance from her fingers.

Varnon continued to feed Vaith, his smile practically lighting up the entire room. Kira suddenly felt his joy overwhelm her. For an instant she saw Vaith through the young man's eyes, the reflection of sunlight on iridescent scales filling her with unbridled happiness. With more effort than necessary, she shoved her mental shields tightly into place, then wiped at the tears that had formed in the corners of her eyes.

"Are you well?" Aertine asked, her voice softer than it

had been at any time Kira could recall.

Kira waved her off. "Yes, of course. My apologies. I've merely been a bit out of sorts these past few days. So much has happened..." She wondered at the rush of emotion. She'd not had such a surge like that from another person before. Was it an effect of the Matriarch's gift that caused her to have opened herself up without warning to another person in such a way? If so, her connections ran even deeper than she'd thought.

"No need to explain," Aertine told her. "We have all had to make...adjustments as of late." She shook her head. "But you did not come here to talk of such things." She lifted the pouch and pulled it open, spilling the contents onto the table.

Vaith stopped eating and cocked a yellow eye at the glittering shards.

"I believe this is what you've come for." Aertine waved a hand over the pile of broken bits. "Though, there is not much I can report."

"May I?" Varnon asked.

Kira glanced at Aertine.

"He is the best apprentice I have trained in all my years," Aertine said. "And he can be trusted not to speak of anything that takes place within this room." She gave him a look that conveyed beyond question that what they discussed here was a secret to be kept, and kept well.

The two women locked eyes for a moment. "If Aertine grants you such trust, then I do as well," Kira said.

"Mind you don't lose any." Aertine told him as he handed Vaith back to Kira.

The little wyvern squawked his displeasure at being separated from his food source, but quieted when Kira shushed him.

With as much eagerness as he'd shown when holding Vaith, Varnon picked up one of the shards and held it to the light that streamed in through the open window. Then he cupped it in his palm and closed his eyes. A moment later, his hand jerked open and he dropped the broken gem onto the table, his eyes wide in startlement.

Aertine leaned forward "What is it?" she demanded. "What did you sense?"

He shook his head. "It wasn't a mere sensation." He held out his hand. His palm was blistered and red where the stone had touched it.

Chapter 14

Aertine grabbed Varnon's wrist and examined the red welt. Her eyes narrowed. "That's a bad burn. You'll need a Physic to keep it from becoming ulcerated."

"Here," Kira said. "Let me tend to that for you. I have a poultice that will help to cool the burn and ease the pain." She reached into the bag at her hip and pulled out the salve container Heresta had gifted her. The feather pattern baked into the clay had been one of the Healer's favorites. She'd loved everything to do with birds. It was the reason Kira had taken to calling her Raven. It had been a joke at first, but Heresta had warmed to the pet name. Kira's heart welled up in remembrance of the old woman. She was glad the jar at least had survived the Sunfleet's shipwreck. She forced herself not to dwell upon it, to push away the thoughts of Milos that always seemed so connected to all else in her mind. Removing the lid, she dipped her fingers into the gray paste.

Varnon's eyes flicked to Aertine who shrugged and loosened her grip from around his wrist so he could extend his hand to Kira. He licked his lips and his face flushed a pretty rose color as Kira placed her cool hand beneath his and examined the wound to be sure there were no particles that might abrade, then gently spread the cream over Varnon's burn.

He flinched at her touch. "Apologies," he murmured.

"A patient need never apologize for expressing pain," Kira quoted one of Heresta's key sayings.

"Thank you," Varnon said, his face taking on a deeper shade of crimson, then relaxing as the salve cooled the burn and worked to alleviate the pain.

"I was not aware you had a Physic's abilities," Aertine said.

Kira shrugged. "I don't. But I was trained as a healer in my...in Aestron. At least, I apprenticed for a time." Thinking of her old life brought a new round of grief to her heart. Heresta had been a keen and demanding teacher, but Kira could certainly use a dose of the old woman's wisdom right now. She let go Varnon's hand and replaced the lid on the salve container. "It will heal more quickly with a Physic's ministrations, but this will at least ease the pain and keep it from worsening in the meanwhile."

Varnon raised his hand in respectful deference. "Thank you, Matriarch."

Kira returned the jar of salve to its place in her pouch and tried not to frown at the title he used. Though it still felt wrong, she needed to get used to it. She had a duty to these people. A responsibility she had been given to protect them and help to heal this land. If a way could be found to do so. "It would be better to seek those ministrations sooner rather than later." She looked pointedly at Aertine. "With the leave of your Mistra, of course."

"Yes. Go."

Varnon seemed about to protest, but Aertine waved him away, her eyes glued to the stone shards that had caused his wound.

*   *   *

"Why do you think that happened?" she asked Kira as soon as Varnon had gone.

"I've no idea." Kira eyed the broken bits, thoughtfully. "Have you had no similar mishap with them?"

Aertine shook her head. "They have hummed with barely the slightest residual power." She held her hand over the broken piece that had burned Varnon. "Nothing like that." She concentrated, lowering her hand closer to the stone bits. "Nothing. Not even the low whisper of energy that was here before."

"May I?" Kira asked.

Aertine pulled away and acquiesced, watching closely for any hint of power that the remains of Kavyn's power stone might reveal.

Hand held above the stone shards, Kira closed her eyes and concentrated. She detected only the faintest bit of energy from them. Vaith opened his wings and let out a squawk of boredom. *Not now*, she sent, pushing him away with her thoughts.

The wyvern hopped from the back of her chair, gliding away from her to land with a clatter on the workbench at the side of the room. Kira opened her eyes and shook her head. "Mind your manners," she told him. "And put that down."

He dropped the shiny polished bit of metal he'd picked up and turned his back on her. She sighed and returned her focus to the work at hand but not before catching a glimpse of a smile fading from Aertine's face.

"You truly do communicate with them as people say." Aertine gestured at the animals. "We have animal adepts, those that can work with animals, fish, or fowl." She shook her head. "But none these days can speak so directly. To communicate as if they understand..."

"They do understand." Kira shrugged. "More or less."

She let her hand fall to her side and slid her fingers across Kelmir's silky head. "As with any true companion, they listen to me when they feel inclined." She jutted her chin at Vaith. "Though, that one is arrogant and has a stubborn streak, as well."

Vaith fluttered his wings and settled down to sulk.

"You see?" Kira gave Aertine a wry smile.

Placing her hand back over the stone shards, she closed her eyes once more and quieted her mind, shutting out her companions and all other distractions. The stone seemed to vibrate below her outstretched palm, but it gave no more sign of energy than that.

She lowered her hand, until it rested directly on top of the jagged bits, but there was no energy exchange, no burning jolt.

Finally, she raised her hand just above the stone bits once more and reached out for the Guardian's line.

The surge of energy that flowed through her and into the stone, slammed her hand away as if it had been slapped and threw the broken bits across the room, causing her eyes to snap open.

Kelmir leaped to his feet, letting out a hiss of displeasure as Vaith zipped out the open window.

Aertine's eyes were round in surprise. Her mouth opened as if she was going to say something, but all that came out was a small outrush of breath and a single word. "Oh."

Kira eyed the palm of her hand. There was no visible sign of any injury or harm. Nor did it feel as if there would be, but a small welt formed on Aertine's left cheek where one of the stone bits must have hit her as it hurled across the room. "My apologies," Kira said. "Had I known of the danger..." She stopped short. "Nay, if anyone should know what kind of danger this stone might cause, it should be me." She reached into the pouch at her waist and took out the container of healing salve and offered it to Aertine, who dipped in a fingertip.

"You…" Aertine searched for words that seemed to evade her, wincing as she applied the medicinal cream to her face. "It's…" Aertine shook her head and gathered herself. "I've never seen it. And…Devira…she never speaks of it." Aertine watched Kira closely, as if she thought she might suddenly rise into the air and float away.

Stunned by the woman's reaction, Kira sat and waited for Aertine to gather her thoughts.

Aertine grew flushed, blood rushing to her face in obvious embarrassment. "I'm so sorry, Matriarch." She tried to stand, sat down again. Held out her hands in formal respect. "We know, we all know, but only the bloodline can connect to source…that way. The rest of us…" she shook her head again in wonder and awe. "Our focus is in what we can connect with, what we can pour something of ourselves into, bits of plant, or stone, or sometimes animals. But what you did…what you do…that is a cut beyond…and I thought, we, some of us, thought…the Guardian's seat… the Matriarch's chains of office…" Flustered, she let her words trail off and dropped her hands. "My apologies. I did not mean to blather."

So. The chill in this woman's manner had been due as much to doubt in Kira's abilities as prejudice against her proclaimed bloodline. "You are not wrong," Kira told her. "The Guardian's seat is the focal point. At least as far as the pillars and the Net, I suppose. The chains… I'm not really certain." She paused, caution causing her to choose her words carefully. She hadn't yet attempted to determine the purpose of the cumbersome chains, nor had she wanted to ask. Her hand involuntarily reached up to her throat. There was something both attractive and yet off-putting about the heavy symbol that had seemed to weigh upon the Matriarch's shoulders in a way that made Kira shudder. In excitement or fear, she still hadn't sorted, but that confusion alone was enough to have kept her from opening herself to them. And more than enough to keep her from allowing the Council to perform the ritual they referred to as the Guardian's Binding. Hence her ongoing denial of the Council's request that she fully embrace her role as Matriarch and Guardian. "At least, as I understand it, that's as it was." She stood, picking up and gathering the broken bits of stone, waving Aertine off as the Mistra rose to aid her.

"The Matriarch...when she lashed back at Kavyn...after he tore down the Net. I don't really know exactly how to describe it, but something shifted." Kira held out her hand to Aertine, pouring the gathered fragments into a small clay tray Aertine had pushed across the table. "She told me it was a gift." She reached over and plucked a bit of glittering stone out of Aertine's auburn hair. "But I don't really see it that way." She peered at the pile of stone chips. "Are you certain you can't mend it?"

Aertine frowned, picked up the tray and poured the stone bits back into the leather pouch, then tucked the bag into a pocket and stood. "Would you come with me?" she asked. "I want to show you something." The angry edge was back in her words, her posture, but there was also a hue of resignation that clung to her.

"Of course." Worry and discomfort pushed at Kira. Where might this woman—who could seem so deferential one moment and so bitterly angry the next—be taking her? She rubbed her fingertips together and glanced over at Kelmir. The big cat tensed his muscles, sensing her unease. Well, she would know soon enough what lay in wait for her. She composed her face into the blank slate she had learned to wear during her brutal years with Toril and followed Aertine out the side door of the workshop and along a well-worn path of smooth stone laid into intricate patterns.

* * *

Kelmir padded close beside Kira, his normal calm still ruffled by the explosion of the stone and her current state of disquiet. The addition of Aertine's anger sent him into a wary protectiveness. Vaith, however, had apparently decided to keep his distance. Likely, he was searching for a small rodent to supplement what he would consider his meager mid-morning bread and cheese. Kira started to reach out and call him to her, but forced herself to let him be. It wasn't fair for her to push her neediness upon her companions. As much as they were an extension of her in so many ways, they were still individuals and needed their freedom and independence.

The path Aertine led her down rambled between overgrown trees and hedges that had likely been well-tended once, but now grew wildly, as if no one cared any longer what happened to this garden. More than once, Aertine held aside a snagging branch to allow Kira passage through the poorly tended greenery.

The mad overgrowth opened out onto a small clearing and Aertine stopped, her shoulders stiff, staring ahead at a large pile of rubble.

"What happened here?" Kira found herself walking forward, drawn to the jumble of broken stones.

"The destruction of our memories. The utter erasure of the Kystrell family's ancestors."

"Your ancestors were entombed here?"

Aertine frowned at her. "Do you not know what a memory keep is?"

Kira shook her head. "I've heard them mentioned since I came to Eilar, but I have not visited one before now. They... they aren't all like this, though, are they?"

"No. They are not." Aertine shook her head, then took in a steadying breath before continuing. "The Eilaran people do not keep the bodies of our dead as some cultures do, but we do store their memories in special places. For our family, it was here, in a carven pillar of marble and hued crystalline."

"We have nothing like that in...where I grew up."

Aertine stared at her in surprise. "How do you recall the past once your elders have passed beyond? How do you keep the moments that changed your family's path? How do you know the stories of your ancestors? Their sorrows? Their joys?" She gazed at the broken remains. "How do you hear their laughter?" Her voice had taken on a sadness that cut Kira to the bone.

"We simply remember them. We all have our memories, do we not?" It sounded weak even to Kira. How long had it been since she could truly remember the shape of her mother's face, or the timbre of her voice? Yet, she had no other answer.

"A memory keep," Aertine said, in the manner of a teacher, "is more than merely a place for storing remembrances. Our ancestors have come here for generations, leaving with us the keys to understanding them. The richness of a memory keep is in the way the memories are shared. Not through a mere telling of story, or sharing of an anecdote, but in a way that can be experienced by those who come after us." Aertine's grew thoughtful. "An intact Memory Keep allows us to hear, to see, those who have passed. They keep such memories alive even after our loved ones have journeyed beyond the veil."

Kira thought of Ardea, of her father—foster-father, she amended. Already, so many things had faded. Her father's laughter was still with her, as was her mother's smile, but the color of his eyes, the shape of her hands. Little things that seemed so insignificant once, now loomed in importance, yet lay beyond recall. A memory keep that could store such things would indeed be a treasure. She gasped when she realized what she was looking at. What had once been a family's memory keep—*her* family's memory keep, she reminded herself—now shattered like the shards in Aertine's pocket. "Was my—your sister, Ardea—were any of her memories...?"

A sad smile broke over Aertine's stern face and her eyes became soft. "Yes."

Kira would give anything to hear her mother's voice again to know something of her past. Sadness and anger filled her. "Who would do such a thing?" she asked in a hushed voice.

"Your mother," Aertine said, her words sharp-edged.

"Ardea?"

"What?" Aertine rounded on her. "Not the woman who raised you. Not my sister. Your real mother. "She quieted her voice before continuing. "Your predecessor. Matriarch Kyrina." She spoke the name, as if it were acid on her tongue. "Our *mad* Matriarch."

Aertine whispered the last so low, Kira was certain it hadn't actually been meant to be heard, at least not by her.

"She did this?" Kira knelt before the wreckage, reaching for a small chunk of shimmering stone, her heart feeling as if it were made of the same stuff at the realization of what had been done here.

"Don't!" Aertine's voice was an angry bark.

"I'm sorry," Kira said. "I meant no disrespect. It's only... I had no idea."

Aertine stared at her. "I thought you knew...that Devira... no, of course she didn't tell you." Aertine shook her head. "She wouldn't have wanted to upset someone in her care."

Kira was surprised at the softness that had crept into Aertine's voice. Rather than an accusation, the comment was delivered as a statement of fact. "I am truly sorry," she told Aertine. "I know what this must mean to you. To your entire family." *And to me.* She wished she could share with Aertine their blood connection, have her aunt understand that she too was grief-stricken by the loss. So many answers. So much history here. So many things about her family that she would never know. "Are all memory keeps made like this one?"

"Many are made of stone, though some families have green places filled with wondrous trees that hold the stories and key moments of their heritage. Some even maintain intricate water displays complete with fountains and the sweet sound of falling and trickling water, though how memories might be stored in liquid is beyond my skill and something I still have trouble comprehending."

Kira leaped up, unable to remain calm. "But you are a stone adept. Surely you could—"

"Do you think I have not tried?" Aertine cut her off angrily. "I've attempted every way I know to repair it. Unsuccessfully, as you can see." She drew in a breath and waved a hand at the wreckage. "Such a simple thing, really. A memory keep." She began to pace. "A container. That's all it is. All it should be. Like a basin or a pitcher." Her hands fidgeted as she walked, cupping together in the shape of a bowl as she said the words. "If you break one, you can piece it back together, patch it well enough and it holds water again. So simple." She dropped her hands to her sides and let out a laugh of frustration. "So simple, and yet, I cannot solve the puzzle of how to remake the container without destroying the contents already within."

Chapter 15

"The soldiers drill daily. The militia grows stronger, but there is something very wrong. We can no longer feel safe from the outside world. Perhaps, this is not such a bad thing. Perhaps it is time to open ourselves up to the larger world, to let in others." Councilor Kersin cast her eyes around the table. The late afternoon sun's rays bathed the Council chamber in a watery light.

"That is not our way!" Councillor Marsal stood halfway out of her seat, hands planted on the polished wooden table and glared at Kersin. Her midnight blue eyes flashed with anger.

Kersin held up a finger to indicate she had not relinquished the floor. "That has not been our way in the past," she corrected. "But the world is changing and, in order to survive, I believe we must change with it." She leaned back in her seat and placed her palms down on the table, signaling that she was finished speaking.

"No. We cannot open ourselves up when we are so defenseless," Marsal retorted.

"Why defenseless? What about the young Matriarch?

Why does she not do her duty? Why will she not assume her rightful place as our Guardian?" Councillor Teldin, the newest among them, asked

"The warding stones are broken," Zoshia replied. "This has been confirmed and is not in question. How then should she protect us? Even upon the seat of power, her reach can be no more than the remains of what was created and has now been destroyed." Zoshia placed her hand palm down on the table.

"But she is of the blood. The land is hers to command. Why does she not simply renew the wards?" Teldin persisted.

"You forget how long she has been gone from this land. Her upbringing in Aestron did not prepare her for this. With no formal training and no living Matriarch to teach and guide her? How should she be able to do what none of us who have lived here our full lives cannot?" Zoshia frowned, surprised at her own words, her defense of this strange young woman about whom she knew so little. Yet, Devira trusted her...

The meeting fell into chaos, Councilors speaking over one another with no pretense of decorum. The afternoon light exhausted itself as they continued to argue, the illumin-crystals on the walls slowly coming to life. A heavy weariness settled onto Zoshia. As the Council Second, she should have more control over the discussion, but her own mind argued with itself, twisting and turning with each new comment. She found it difficult to side with the Matriarch, yet more so to side against her.

"But she is the Matriarch. And we have no other. If she cannot defend our land and people, we will be at the mercy of the outsiders." Teldin insisted.

"Why then would you have us invite the wolf directly into our home and then expect him not to kill and eat our sheep?" demanded Marsal, raising her voice to be heard over the rest.

The First raised his hand and clamped his fingers into

a fist. "Enough."

The voices fell silent.

The First dropped his hand and opened his palm in Zoshia's direction, allowing her the opportunity to present her final views as Second. She shifted in her seat, her weariness churning to frustration at her own ambivalence on the matter, then laid her open hands upon the table, palms up. "I have no answer for you." She gazed around at the haggard faces.

"What then shall we do?" Their newest member, a young music adept named Vestyne, voiced the question that resonated in all their minds.

The exasperation that showed clear in the First's face reflected all of their thoughts and Zoshia's mind raced for answers, but nothing came back to her. Nothing, except the warm flush that threatened to overtake her when she thought of Devira, and the chill that reached for her heart at the thought of what this threat to Eilar might mean for them all.

Chapter 16

Devira rose, dressing quickly and closing the sleeping room door behind her as she stole into the main room. She savored the comfort of the familiar normalcy. With their odd hours keeping them awake at such differing times, she had often found herself moving silently through their chambers to keep from waking Zoshia. As quietly as possible, she stoked the fire and filled the small kettle with water, swinging it over the growing flames to heat. She sat for a moment upon the warming hearth, feeling relaxed and rested for the first time since the awful day she and Zoshia had parted so harshly.

"Up so early?" a sleepy voice said from behind her.

She smiled, shifting to watch as her lifemate crossed the room to sit beside her on the thick rug.

"I was going to bring you your tea in bed," she said. "But now you've gone and wasted your chance."

"Ah, well. It was a kind thought." Zoshia sighed, wrapping an arm around Devira's shoulders and hugging her gently to her. "I've an early Council meeting, though."

"Oh? Has anything happened?" She forced herself to

keep from exposing her deep curiosity. Zoshia had ever been closed about Council business. It was a rare moment when she shared with Devira the things that were discussed within that chamber. Though, now there were even more secrets between them, secrets that worked both ways. She shifted back to the fire, watching the flames eat away at the wood, darkening the fuel as it devoured it.

Zoshia stifled a yawn. "Nothing has changed that I am aware of. Our new Matriarch refuses to perform the binding ritual, acquiescing only so far as to sit upon Guardian's seat and wear the chains of office as an actor dons a costume. The Council cannot continue to accept such a sham." She sat back and gazed into Devira's eyes. "I know I promised not to push, but if you can recall anything else about that night. Anything that might help us to understand."

Devira shrugged and looked away. "I told you all I can. There are still holes in my mind from the fall." She resisted the urge to place her hands upon her skull. The bones had reknitted, but her memories had not. "The Matriarch is the one to whom you should put your questions."

Zoshia frowned. "Our new Matriarch has no love of the Council, as you know."

"You cannot blame her, after what she was put through. The Interrogation?" Devira heard the accusation in her tone, but it was too late to take it back.

"No," Zoshia replied. "You are right. I cannot blame her, but under the circumstances, with all the evidence against her—"

"Evidence? Lies and accusations are not evidence."

"The Council did what we thought was warranted." Zoshia placed her fingertips upon Devira's cheek and angled her face so their eyes met. "I was hoping that perhaps as her caregiver, you might..."

Devira stared at her mate, appalled. "You, of all people, know that would be a breach of my oath." She pulled away.

"Devira, please," Zoshia pleaded. "I'm not asking you to

betray a confidence. Nor to do anything that goes against your oath. Only, if you could ask her to speak with us. To share..."

Devira rose to her feet, uncertain whether the heat she felt came from the closeness to the fire, or the anger that spilled through her. "Did you seek me out yestereve merely to push me to pry my patient for information you might then share with the Council?"

"No," Zoshia insisted. "That wasn't it at all."

"No?" Devira stared down at her. "But you could hardly wait until we'd even broken our first fast together before asking me to badger a patient in my care. One who has already been traumatized over and again."

Zoshia reached for her, but Devira backed away.

"I don't know you, anymore, Zoshia Valpine." She strode across the room, heading for the sleeping room, but stopped in the doorway and rounded on her lifemate. "I wonder if I ever did." She closed the door behind her, leaving a startled Zoshia alone beside the steaming kettle.

Chapter 17

Kira pulled the tiniest thread of power, tugging it bit by bit toward the stone before her. She stared at the crystal, focused all her thoughts on it, pressing against the hard surface with her mind. Over and over again, the material rejected her, slapping back at her, the line of power snapping back to its source.

The walls of her room pressed in on her and she sat back, exhausted. How had the Matriarch managed to contain the power she had used. How did she control it? "If I can't do this, if I can't control this tiny bit of power, how can I ever help these people?"

She thought back to her lessons with her mother Ardea, the way she taught her to go deep, to dive below the surface of the water. "But that was different." The complaint in her own voice made her cringe. Now, in lesson after lesson, children succeeded where she failed to progress.

Vaith squawked and Kira recognized the echo of her frustration and sighed. "How can I possibly penetrate below the surface of stone?"

She dropped her hand down and sank her fingers into

Kelmir's warm fur. Her two companions were constant and reassuring, but they offered her no help with this task. Her skills with animals were vastly different from what she was attempting here. They were open to her, wanted to allow her to connect with them, meeting her halfway. Right now, they would clearly rather be out in the fields, hunting, or merely taking in the green forest and the open sky. As would she. And why not? In order to set herself at ease for this task, Kira needed to clear her mind. What better way to do so?

She rose and crossed the room and opened the door, so intent on her goal, she nearly ran into the Council First, Meryk, who stood in the hallway.

"Matriarch?" his voice was a question, but it was clear he'd been headed to see her. "I would have asked for a meeting in the Guardian's Chamber, as is protocol, but I discovered the Seat empty again." His tone remained neutral, but his words implied a rebuke.

What did he want from her? An apology? After all the Council had put her through? And what would be the point of sitting on that hard seat when the land's protections lay in ruin? Kira held her tongue and extended her hands in respect, but not deference, refusing to give him the satisfaction he sought and showing no concern for his comment. "The Council seems to have our day-to-day affairs well in hand." She ushered Vaith and Kelmir out into the hall and shut the door of her chamber behind them, a not so subtle way of communicating her unwillingness to entertain more than a hurried discussion with the First.

"Are you headed somewhere?" he asked, as if there remained some question about her intentions.

Or maybe he was hoping she would change her mind and invite him in? But there was no way she could stay cooped up a moment longer. She needed time and space in which to allow her mind to work on the problem indirectly. "I need some fresh air and sunshine. It's far too stuffy in here." She smiled, wondering if he'd catch the implied insult, a small part of her rather hoping he would.

But the Council First was either beyond the gibe or too skilled at this sort of banter to let anything she said register on his face. "Perhaps, I could walk with you." He tapped his walking stick lightly against the stone floor. "I have something I wish to discuss."

"Actually," Kira said brightly, "I am heading for the stables. Trad needs the workout." And frankly so do I, she thought. *Vaith, Kel, meet me at the stables.*

Kelmir eyed the First, huffed out a grunt and padded away. Vaith circled once, then followed Kelmir down the hallway that led to the keep's rear exit. The First watched them go, his brow wrinkled in thought.

"Do you ride, First Meryk?" Kira asked with feigned politeness.

"Not in some time, no." His face flickered a hint of annoyance before returning to the blank slate he normally wore. "However, I will accompany you as far as the stable, if you would be so inclined." He waved her forward.

"Of course," Kira said. Part of her, the part that hated having to play this role—the part that flinched at the edge of memory recalling her time with Toril and the way she'd had to always navigate his moods in order to attempt to protect herself—wished that instead of acquiescing she could simply say no. On the other hand, she had committed herself to this path by her own choice. Would she always live to regret her choices? But no, being with Milos had not been regrettable. It was the shortness of their time together that caused the heartache at the path she had chosen. Though, the way they had parted was another matter that continued to incite remorse.

How had she come to this place in her life where she felt obligated to settle the troubles of an entire people?

"Now that you have had time to mourn your mother," the old man said, "the Council expects you would have made some effort to adjust to your new role, to settle in to the duties and responsibilities inherent in that role. Therefore," he cleared his throat, "I have come to you in my capacity as Council First to request that you take your proper place on the Guardian's Seat as the dictates of Eilaran convention require, to properly perform the Guardian's Binding. Also, the Council will want your answer sooner rather than later, and I was hoping I might be able to convey your response personally."

As he finished speaking, they passed through the archway that led from the main keep out to the ante yard. The silence stretched between them and, with a start, Kira realized that while they had been walking slowly through the hallways, she'd been so lost in her own thoughts she had completely missed the full impact of what the First had been saying. "Answer?"

"If you choose to accept the Council's request, we will move forward with the formalities. The Binding ritual. If not...well, let us not speak of that." He continued walking without looking at her, his gaze focused on the ground before him as he planted the tip of his walking stick securely with each step before leaning on it.

Kira stopped moving.

The First paused and shifted to face her. "We need our Matriarch. It has been some time since your predecessor was able to adequately manage her duties, aside from maintaining the land's defenses, and your participation will reestablish some normalcy for all of us. Despite your reticence to assume your place upon the Guardian's Seat, the Council has determined that this is necessary and insists on your quick action in this regard. In addition, you must immediately familiarize yourself with the ongoing business and governance of our people."

Kira felt the sting of guilt in his words. She had been avoiding her responsibilities. With Milos gone, she had wanted to be left to herself. She had assumed this role, she chided herself—albeit accepting it as an obligation due to the Matriarch's legacy, one Kira had not asked for—with the goal of helping these people to reestablish their defenses. She had not given much thought to the ruling of an entire country. She blanched at the thought of it. Yet, as much as she desired to be elsewhere, this commitment needed to be fulfilled. At least, until she could find a way to transition the Matriarch's power to someone better suited to the role, if possible. But how could she manage that when her abilities were so devoid of usefulness despite the power the Matriarch had bestowed upon her? Especially when there were so few skilled adepts to choose from. And how then to transfer the power she had inherited when she had so little understanding of it? The thought stunned her.

Clearly, she hadn't thought things through when she had obligated herself to this path. Would there ever be a day when she could leave this land in more capable hands? Or would she be resigned to spend her days here? Ruling alone? Perhaps losing herself to it as had Matriarch Kyrina?

No. She refused to think about what it might mean to be forever anchored to this place and position. There must be another option. Even when things appeared hopeless, as if there was no way out, there was always another option. Heresta had shown her that. She only needed to figure out what it was.

Meanwhile, she needed to learn the things her mother had not had the time to teach her and, to do that, she must begin by acting like the ruler she was supposed to be. "Yes," she said, as much to convince herself as to provide a response to his inquiry.

The First jerked his shaggy old head, surprise registering on his features for the first time Kira could recall since meeting him. "Yes?"

"Yes." Kira gazed at the old man and raised a hand to her heart. "Soon. For today, I need some time to reflect on...personal matters." She waved a hand in the direction of the stable.

Vaith and Kelmir waited by the big open barn door, the small wyvern flying back and forth, teasing the big cat by swooping low to drag his tail across Kelmir's head. Kel grumbled, flicking his ears in irritation, but otherwise ignored Vaith's playfulness. This small bit of normalcy in Kira's odd new life caused both a sliver of joy and a slice of pain to cut across her emotions.

The First leaned against his walking stick and raised his hand in deference to her. "I shall inform the Council, then." He nodded in a knowing way with what seemed to be a flicker of wry humor crossing his wrinkled old face.

Kira wondered for a brief instant if he knew that her words were but an excuse to put him off once more, that she had still not convinced herself to walk forward on this path she had chosen, but she schooled her features. "First Meryk." With a flick of her hands, she gestured her intent to take her leave, then strode off after her companions, finally opening herself up to their elation at the aspect of heading out into the forest.

Though all of her key mental barriers remained in place, she sensed the First watching her with curiosity. But behind that lurked something else. Something that did not seem to come from him, yet felt as if it were somehow riding on the edge of his consciousness.

Or hers.

Kira shivered, despite the warmth of the afternoon sun, and marched into the stable. She threw a smile and a wave to the groom, who left off his task of cleaning and polishing tack and grabbed Trad's bridle from its place on the wall. "Good day, Matriarch," he nearly sang the cheery greeting. "Your gray will be happy to see you. I believe he has tired of me and my paltry attentions." He grinned as he said it, letting Kira know he'd given Trad plenty of riding and grooming time.

"More likely he's grown fat and lazy with you spoiling him terribly every second I'm out of view." As the scent of oiled leather and fresh hay curled itself into her brain, Kira recalled a distant stable and a much younger groom, Harl. How, she wondered, were Harl and Milvari and Brilissa and all the rest of the people she'd come to care for at Tem Hold? Had she known that leaving them behind would be permanent, would she have chosen to ride out that day? Sadly, she knew the answer to this question, as much as it pained her to admit it. She had been driven by a deep-seated need to know who she really was and where she'd come from. And now she knew. Though, in many ways, the answers were as confusing and off-putting as had been the not knowing.

Beware the questions that drive hardest, for their answers often hide the longest barbs. It seemed there was always a place for Heresta's wisdom.

Kira gazed around the stable, so much larger and better appointed than that of Tem Hold. And yet, she thought, this place was not better. Nor, as much as she liked him, was this groom a better man than she was certain Harl was growing to be. She recalled how the young stableman's apprentice had watched and waited, holding vigil with her as she worked to clean the terrible wound Trad had received during their battle with a rock troll.

She shuddered at the recollection of her hard-won victory that stormy night and the way she'd nearly lost Trad to the poison from the rock troll's vicious claw. Instead, she shifted her thoughts to the ride ahead.

The groom grabbed Trad's tack and headed into the stall.

Vaith followed, flying a zigzag pattern through the cool shadows of the stable to land on the stall door. Trad nickered in recognition and stomped his nervous excitement as the groom opened the door and slipped a halter over his head. "There you are," he said. "Your mistress is here for you, so you can stop complaining, now."

Kira bit her lower lip, certain the words were not meant

for her, but taking them to heart anyway. She'd spent little to no time with Trad since arriving on Eilar. Admittedly, the first weeks of that time apart had been no fault of her own. With the loss of her memories in the island's fog, she'd completely forgotten everything and everyone, including Trad.

But since the battle with Kavyn in the Guardian's Room, though there had been ample time for her to spend with her horse, she'd found excuses not to do so. Being around Trad reminded her too much of her time traveling with Milos. It wasn't that she was trying to forget that time. Only that the memories made it harder for her to avoid the urge to run after him, to beg to go with him back to Aestron. Now that the Gilded Hawk had left port, as much as those memories still tugged at her heart, there was no longer any way for her to change course.

Milos was gone, and she was here, in Eilar, and would remain so for as long as it took to reestablish the safety net these people needed. Or until such time as they no longer needed one at all, if it please Troka.

"He's more than happy to see you," the groom told her from inside the stall.

"And I am happy to see him, as well. I should not have stayed away so long," Kira said by way of apology to Trad and, at the same time, an explanation to the man who cared for him in her stead.

She waited as the groom finished saddling Trad, then led him out to her, handing her the reins before offering his cupped hands to help her into the saddle.

"Thank you." She rubbed her knuckles against Trad's neck, smiling as he shook his mane out happily. Then she reached for the pommel and, though she didn't really need it, with the groom's help, she slid into the saddle.

"The new leather is still a bit stiff," the groom told her. "But your old saddle, or what was left of it, had seen much better days. Despite the fair skills of the adept who created and tooled it, this one will take a bit more breaking in, but once done I think you'll be pleased with the comfort Eilaran tack offers."

"Thank you, I'm sure I will," Kira said, wondering if she were being honest with the man. The Aestron saddle she had grown accustomed to was sturdy and functional. As pretty as it was, with its swirling embellishments and gleaming buckles, she wasn't sure the Eilaran saddle and bridle would stand up to the wear and tear of heavy riding. Though, in circumspect, she realized there wouldn't be much time for that. As a fully bound and committed Matriarch, she'd be expected to do a lot of things, but spending her days out riding was more than likely not included in that long list of items.

She peered out the stable door at the slant of the afternoon sun. She had better be going if she wanted to get any enjoyment out of what remained of the day. With a nod to the groom, she squeezed her knees against Trad's sides, guiding him out of the stable and into the bright sunlight. Once outside, she gave him a tap of her heel and they were off. Kelmir loped ahead and Vaith fluttered and swooped in and out of the branches as they left the stable and gardens behind them and galloped under the dappled shade of the orchards that ringed the keep.

Like old times, Kira thought, though there was now a hole in her heart, one that—as much as she loved them all—Vaith, Trad, and Kelmir could not completely fill.

Chapter 18

"Physica Devira sent you a special tea." Kelliss placed
the pot and cup on the table beside the fire.

Kira placed a hand on her belly. "I've not been hungry.
I doubt even tea will sit well."

Kelliss flicked her eyes to the hand on her midriff.
Something in the way the apprentice Physica continued
to regard her made Kira self-conscious, and she quickly
took her hand away. "I'm not used to being waited upon.
Nor to the worries of ruling," she murmured in the way of
an excuse. It was true she'd been unable to adjust to her
role as Matriarch, and continued to delegate much of the
day-to-day decision making to the Council. A move they
had at first acceded to, after Kira had pointed out that
they had been doing much of such work even before the
death of the former Matriarch due to her state of mind. But
now that she had committed to taking up the Matriarch's
mantle, her responsibilities would increase. She began to
understand how Milos must have felt when thrust into the
role of Tem Hold's ruler. No wonder he'd been so dour when
first they'd met.

"Devira suggested you make an effort to drink this." The woman filled a cup with the steamy liquid. "I think you will be pleasantly surprised at how well it sits with you, and it will help to build your strength." She handed the cup to Kira, who sniffed at the contents suspiciously and wrinkled her nose at the bitter odor.

"What is in this? It smells of peppermint and sweetginger."

"You've a good nose." The woman said in a matter-of-fact tone.

Kira sipped the brew and made a face. "It could use some honey to sweeten it. And is that ellsberry leaf?"

"You've also a trained palate." Kelliss nodded.

"But..." Kira paused. "This tea is normally made for women who are with..." She nearly dropped the cup, as the truth of her condition sank in.

The apprentice tilted her head to one side, a knowing smile turning up the corners of her mouth. "I'll just pop down to the kitchen and fetch you some honey for your tea," she said as she slipped out the door.

Kira set the cup onto the table and slumped into her chair, the enormity of her situation hitting her like a tidal wave.

Milos was gone, and here she was, in a land of mostly strangers, carrying his child. And there was no way for him to know.

Perhaps, it was better that he didn't. He might have felt it necessary to stay, and she knew that was not what he'd wanted. No, the news of a growing child would have complicated things between them even more than they already were. She would need to bear this burden herself.

And not everyone here was a stranger. Devira, at least, she could call a friend, if not Aertine. But would the Eilaran people, who seemed to care so much about blood and bloodlines, accept this child? This babe of another land? Would they accept that Kira was now a mother? Would the fact that she had no official consort concern them? The attending Physica seemed unconcerned about it. But would the Council be as accepting? They had all been civil to her, if not overly warm, but what were the laws and protocols of such a thing?

So many questions she needed to ask. Not only of Devira but of herself. She placed her hand back upon her middle. Was there truly life growing inside her? Was it possible that she could be a mother? Her memories rolled back to her own childhood. A vision of her mother Ardea, who had been firm but tender, warm yet strong-willed, so many aspects of personality seemed beyond a single person. Would Kira be able to embrace motherhood? Could she wear so many faces? How did someone become everything necessary to provide a child all it would need and deserve?

It wasn't as if she had never considered the idea of a child. But she had always rejected the thought. And how could she be everything a child needed a mother to be? Alone in this land? With the ugliness of the recent past, her own family's turmoil, and the political landscape still so uncertain? And how could she expose a child to the expectations of an entire people? Not to mention the overarching lie of who she really was. A usurper to the Guardian's seat.

She glowered at the cooling tea. There wasn't enough honey on the entire island to sweeten this cup.

Chapter 19

Milos shivered in the cool air. The pitch-black night pressed against him, as it if had substance. Somewhere in the darkness, a child cried. Its pitiful wail tore claws of sorrow across his heart. He crept forward in the darkness, following the sound. His fist was closed around something cool and solid, and he raised his hand and rolled it open. Something glimmered on his outstretched palm. Light streamed from it and a pale glow filled the darkness. Ahead, a woman sat upon the ground, swaying slowly back and forth. He crept nearer. As the woman rocked, the glowing light shimmered off her red hair. "Kira?"

The woman didn't turn, but continued to move in a hypnotic way with her back to him, something small and mewling cradled in her arms.

Milos woke with a start, unsure of what had awakened him from the dream until he heard something moving in the dark. He shifted his weigh to slip out of his hammock. Beside him, Dahl cried out as a dark shadow slid between them and the hatch. A heavy object skimmed the side of Milos's head, knocking him back. He fell against the hammock, barely disentangling himself in time to avoid being clobbered with a wooden belaying pin.

Something thudded to the deck and the shadow wielding the pin yelped. The man cursed, hissing in pain and dropped his weapon, falling hard against the bulkhead with a thump. Their sleeping quarters were suddenly filled with fighting, shouting men. The darkness made it impossible to tell friend from foe, though Milos knew he and Dahl were alone and being targeted. He must find the boy and protect him.

"Dahl!" Milos called.

"Here," Dahl's voice came back to him, breaking high with fear.

At least the boy was still alive and conscious. Milos tried to make his way through the press of bodies to where the boy's voice had come from. Someone kicked him in the knee and he went down, attempting to roll out of the way of too many stomping, scuffling feet. Something fell from Milos' hand, flaring brightly as it rolled across the deck, then went out leaving a deeper darkness behind. He reached for it, his fingers closing tightly around the smooth piece of crystal.

"What was that?" someone hissed.

"Leave it."

Milos recognized the First Mate's raspy voice.

"Milos!" Dahl's muffled cry was filled with panic.

"Shut it!" the mate growled in the darkness. "Wake the rest of the crew and it will go worse for you."

Milos rolled into a kneeling position and jabbed a fist upward, catching someone in the stomach. The man he'd hit yelped in pain and fell back. It gave Milos enough room to slip aside and rise. In the dark space, shadows moved against blackness, making it impossible to discern who he was fighting, but Milos didn't have to see them to know the crew of the Sunfleet were to blame for the ruckus. He punched blindly in the dark, keeping his reach high enough to avoid hitting Dahl, ducking between strikes in the hope of making himself less of a target. With any luck, he could trick the assailants into injuring one another and reduce their numbers, or at least slow their attack. Some of his blows slid off cheek and chin, but others landed solidly and the scuffling men began to give ground.

A lucky punch clipped Milos in the side of the head, knocking him into a coil of rope that slid down over his head and shoulder. He tried to free himself, but before he could, he was grabbed and thrown to the floor. He was pummeled with fists and feet. Someone connected a kick to his side and a searing pain shot through his ribcage. He doubled up, covered his head with his arms and tried to roll onto his knees. Someone crashed down onto his back, reaching an arm around his neck.

He heard Dahl struggling nearby and a surge of anger flashed through him. He let out an angry shout and heaved the combatant off his back. The man flew across the small space and collided with another.

Suddenly, Dahl was yelling, men were cursing. A lamp blazed against the open hatch, casting light onto the chaos in the hold.

"Now you've done it," the First Mate growled. He took the opportunity to land a final punch to Milos's midsection as the hold filled with Eilaran crew. They restrained the angry Aestrons who had attacked Milos and the boy.

When they were brought before the Eilaran captain, Milos considered asking for leniency for the mate and his men, but he knew nothing he did would be appreciated. Besides, one look at the bruises already beginning to discolor Dahl's pale face in the lantern light, filled Milos with rage. He stood silent, arms crossed over his heaving chest, as Captain Jayvel questioned the men who had been a part of the chaos.

The captain looked as if he had been roused from a deep slumber, or perhaps had not had any sleep at all. He stifled a yawn before pointing to the Aestron mate, Stronar.

"You've been aching for trouble since you came aboard," he accused.

Stronar glared back at him. "We've been given more trouble than ever we cared to have," he grumbled. "We're owed, and not been paid, and now we're expected to work for passage while this one rides along like some sort of Holder."

"So, you thought to attempt to turn bruises into coin?" the captain asked.

The other Aestron crewmembers stared at their feet, but the mate kept his eyes glued to the captain's, his mouth cut like a scar across his angry face.

"Falder," the captain called out.

"Aye, Captain," an Eilaran sailor responded.

"When you signed to the Hawk, were you promised pay for your service?"

"Aye, sir." The tall crewman bobbed his head.

"And were we to be shipwrecked and I perhaps lost, what would be your recourse as one of the survivors?"

"To be grateful for my life, first off." The Eilaran gave the Aestrons a meaningful look. "Then to be glad of any healing or sustenance offered me."

"And what of passage back to your homeland? How might that be accomplished?"

"I'd expect to work my way," the sailor said. "And once home, I'd thank the stars and our ancestors I had made it home safe before seeking recompense from any surviving ship's owners."

The captain placed one hand on the ship's railing, patting it as one might gentle a favorite mount. "A sensible approach," he said, looking out at the dark water that churned to froth at the ship's passing. "Though, we all hope that is never a path you will find yourself navigating."

"Aye, sir." The sailor put a fist to his chest.

Stronar grunted. "Easy to say, when you're standing sound on the deck of a sturdy ship. But we ain't been so lucky." He waved at his men. "And the captain of the Sunfleet hadn't got no kin that we know of. The ship and all its cargo were lost. So, as you can see, we've got nothin' in return for our service. And no expectations of any."

The Aestrons shuffled their feet and mumbled in agreement.

"That does not mean you have nothing more to lose." Captain Jayvel shook his head. "Short rations for three days," he ordered, then glanced over at Dahl, whose swollen lip and blackened eye shone in the flickering light. "See to it that they are all visited by the ship's Physic first, especially the boy." He glared at Stronar. "And since we have no official holding cell on this vessel, I want this one sequestered in the storage hold for that time."

Stronar spat on the deck.

Captain Jayvel glared at the angry Aestron, his tired eyes fierce in the lamplight. "After he scrubs my deck." He spun on his heel and retired to his cabin, boot heels resounding sharply against the wooden deck.

The mate looked to his crewmembers for support, but the Eilaran crew herded them back below decks at the same time as someone shoved a bucket at him.

He scowled at the man before ripping the bucket out of his hands, then he turned on Milos and sneered. "This isn't finished," he growled. "Not by far."

Chapter 20

Kira puzzled over the riddle of the memory keep. She rose from her seat beneath the jesmapine tree and followed the path to the water's edge. Kelmir, sleeping in a pool of sunlight, barely stirred, watching her through a single slitted eye. Vaith fluttered down from the branch where he'd been perched, swooped down and circled her until she paused and held out her arm to him. Normally the little wyvern was a welcome distraction, but today so many things preyed on her mind, she wasn't in the mood. So, when he lit upon her wrist, she coerced him up to her shoulder where he could tuck himself beside her ear and wrap his tail around the back of her neck, leaving her to her thoughts.

She watched the stream flow past, slipping by the grassy banks and thought again how someone might infuse water with a memory. Stone and tree, solid objects, she could understand, but water? What if it spilled out? Or dried up? What then would happen to the memories within?

She stopped in her tracks. What if the memories within the keeps were all stored within them as if liquid? What if, instead of repairing the broken stone, the memories could somehow be poured into a new container? Had it been attempted before?

She reached into the pouch that hung from the strap slung across her shoulder and pulled out one of the glittering light stones. The smooth round globe was polished to a high sheen, but no light came from within it. An empty vessel, it waited for the touch of a skilled hand to fill it with radiance. Or, Kira thought, perhaps fill it with something else?

She had to speak to Aertine and Devira.

Chapter 21

He was in that place again, moving through the glistening fog, which sparkled with reflected sunlight that refused to pierce the thick vaporous cloud. A humming sound drew him and the mists separated to become the night sky overhead, the sparkling of stars twinkled at him from the velvet blackness of this new place. Beneath his feet, the ground mirrored the sky to dizzying effect until he no longer knew which way was up or down, only that he needed to keep moving forward to keep from falling through into another place, and he needed to remain here.

"Milos." The voice whispered past him on an eddying breeze, pulling him forward with it until he stood before a familiar stone pillar.

"I know this place." He reached out a hand and placed it upon the stone surface. The rough texture radiated heat beneath his fingers, making him shiver with the realization that the dark night around him was cold enough to steal the warmth from his body.

"I'm glad you came," Kira said, stepping out from behind the pillar and   placing her hand over his. Heat flowed from her fingers, flared up his arm and into his breast. "I've missed you."

He squeezed his eyes shut against the vision of her, his chest tight.

"Milos, open your eyes. I need to speak with you." She reached up with her other hand and placed her fingers on his cheek. "I'm sorry I said those things. I was stupid and stubborn—"

"I wish you were real," he heard himself say as he pulled his hand from beneath hers and let the swirling mists float him up and away.

"I am." The words spun away from him.

He tried to reach back, to keep himself from moving farther away from her, but he found himself slung across time and space, landing with a start.

He opened his eyes to peer around in the darkness.

There was something about the experience that unraveled him. His hand felt cold and he tucked it beneath the thick woolen blanket. He pulled the dream closer, examining it. It had seemed so real. Kira had seemed so solid.

He wanted to believe her.

But here he was, swaying in a hammock, the snores and grunts of other men surrounding him. He lay wide awake, aboard the Gilded Hawk and bound for home. Dreams of Kira haunting him. How long, he wondered, would it be before he lost even that?

Chapter 22

Marquon stood beside the stream, its water darkening in the fading light. A light footstep behind him caused him to tense, but he did not turn to greet the newcomer. "If your errand is not important, I'd like this time for solace."

"If solace is your need, perhaps you'd like to unburden your thoughts." Tesalin came to stand beside him.

They'd been friends and companions since their youth. But the thoughts and worries that skittered through his mind were still a tangle of seemingly disconnected threads. "Not like another can unravel this knot for me."

"Well, then, perhaps you should see a mentalist?" Her tone was light, chiding, an attempt to get a rise from him.

"It won't work," he said. "Not for this. But I thank you for your guidance." He knew she was concerned about him, else she would not have bothered to follow him away from the training compound, but he was unable to put her mind at rest; his own was such a flurry of doubt and worry. "You needn't be overwrought on my behalf." It was an old joke between them, but this evening it fell as flat as his spirits.

"Ah, well, the river is lovely to watch. But I thought your

meditations were more physically oriented."

He let loose a small laugh.

"At least I can still give you cause for mirth." Tesalin picked up a pebble from the bank and bounced it on the palm of her hand before tossing it into the stream.

They stood in silence as the small splash disappeared. The river continued to flow as usual, without any hint of the disturbance the small stone had made.

"Will we leave a trace?" Marquon murmured.

"You know we do." Tesalin insisted, sounding surprised that anyone might ask such a question. "We have our friends." She elbowed him. "And we have the memory keeps."

"And if we do not contribute to them before...before our passing? What happens after our friends and family have joined our ancestors?"

"You're thinking of your nephew? The one who was lost. And that boy the Aestron saved."

"Perhaps. But not only them." Marquon bent down and picked up a stone of his own and held it between thumb and forefinger, staring at it in the evening light.

"A single pebble means nothing to the river, but it can mean a great deal to a man with no shoes." Tesalin's voice was low, flat, as if she were recalling and repeating something she had heard somewhere many years before.

He glanced at her in surprise. "Since when do you quote the philosophers?"

"Since about the same time that you began to keep your worries of the Outlanders in your own pocket."

"Fair enough." He shifted his stance, settling further into his thoughts. "Why do you think they sent such a small force? Was it a test? Of us? Or of the Net? And how did they know to test it on that day?"

"You think too much on such things. The question we need to be asking is when will they come again?"

"I agree with you on that point, at least." He gave a small

nod before throwing the stone into the stream.

"And when they do come, what do they intend?" she added as the stone slipped beneath the water.

"What all conquerors intend, of course, to destroy and pillage. In the end," he shook his head, "to conquer."

"Yes, but why now? Has the timing of their attack not given you pause? They come at us right after our missing Matriarchess returns?"

"What are you saying?"

"Think on it," Tesalin urged. "Her return has brought nothing but destruction: the death of the Matriarch, an attack by the Outlanders, and the mangling of her brother's mind. And now she prepares to sit upon the Guardian's Seat. I hear the ritual binding will take place soon. All this in the span of less than a quarter turn. Does that not raise more questions for you?"

A chill ran across Marquon's skin. What Tesalin was suggesting... Could it possibly be true? Yes, all of these things came about after the Matriarchess had returned to Eilar. And, after her ascent to the Guardian's Seat was secured, she had allowed Milos, a man she had professed to love to easily separate from her. Was there deeper deceit involved as Tesalin suggested? Or was his lifelong friend falling prey to seeing conspiracy and deception where none existed? "I see no proof beyond happenstance that these things have all come to pass at the same time as her return. Besides, Milos, who helped us to turn back the attack, thought well of her. She even offered him a place as her consort."

Tesalin let out a snort of derision. "Would you wish to go from an equal partner to something less?"

He knew her thoughts on this matter, and agreed in theory, though in actuality he preferred things the way they were, believed in the supportive nature of the Consort's role and the nurturing aspect of their historically Matrilineal rulers. But now was not the time to argue politics. Besides, they had covered this ground as well as trileaf moss covered the riverbank in early spring. Neither of them had ever yielded on the subject. Nor did he expect they would now.

The silence stretched out as the river flowed past and the last of the sun's rays slid into darkness. Finally, Marquon found his voice. "No, I suppose I would not wish to change positions in such a way. Though, for the right person." He winked at her. Another running jest between them.

She snorted. "We both know I'm not designed to your preferences."

He sobered again. "But Milos is our proven ally and he placed all his trust in her."

"Of course, he did," Tesalin retorted. "But that was before they came to our shores, and the world changed for us all."

"I trust him, and I trust his judgment."

"Men are ever the worst judges of women, especially men in love," Tesalin murmured, tossing another stone into the dark water.

Chapter 23

"Sail, ho!" called the ship's lookout.

"At what reckoning?" asked the Second Officer.

"Two points abaft the beam, portside, three, maybe four, leagues off, but coming fast."

"Of what origin?" hollered the Captain's Second.

"It's gray sails, Sir!"

Captain Jayvel glanced up, startled. "Outlanders? How many?"

"The lookout says a single ship. Makes it a fast mariner by her cut."

"A fast mariner? What the ashes are they doing in these waters this time of season?"

"No idea, Captain." The Second Officer stood by, ready for orders. He kept his voice even, but his face registered concern. "Could they be planning another attack on Eilar?"

The captain rubbed his chin in thought. "Not likely with a single ship this far out and following, but perhaps..." He stared in the direction the lookout had indicated. "What prize are you after?" he murmured.

"We could try giving them a run and see. If they pursue,

maybe it's simple piracy they're about. If not..." A muscle twitched in the Second's jaw.

Captain Jayvel grimaced. "Unfurl the airsails," he commanded, his voice calm, but his demeanor taut. "And call up the airslingers." The Second Officer repeated his commands, calling across the decks to the crewmembers, who snapped to, leaping into action. The Gilded Hawk was a single-masted schooner equipped with the standard square sails for a vessel its size, but included two additional masts set at angles beside the standard main mast.

Milos watched in wonder as two new sails unfurled in addition to the sails the ship was already flying. They were oddly shaped, triangular with rounded corners, and made of something that appeared finer than canvas, yet dropped into place with a sturdy snap.

Two Eilarans took their places on the deck. One, a tall woman with short-cropped hair, stood directly beneath the odd starboard sail. The other, a thin man with wild hair that stuck out from his round head in every direction, took his place below the new port sail.

"Airslingers ready," called the Second Officer, standing between the two.

Both of the airslingers closed their eyes.

"How on the approach?" called up the Captain.

"Still coming on direct, Captain," shouted the lookout. "They've closed the distance to near two leagues."

"Begin." The captain said. "Slow to the rise, then add on. Let's see if we can get them to give up what they're on about."

"Begin," repeated his Second. "Slow to the rise, then up."

The airslingers riased their hands and the extra sails billowed out, filling with a wind that had not previously existed, and the sloop leaped forward over the dark water.

"Now, we shall see," murmured the captain. He shifted his attention to the gray sails that had grown closer while they put their energies into increasing the sloop's speed.

The Outlander ship pursued them, still closing the distance.

The Captain seemed surprised. "Have the airslingers double their efforts," he called out. "And ready the defenses."

"Aye, Captain," shouted his Second Officer.

The additional sails filled then flagged as if the air that filled them grew and ebbed at turns. The Captain glared at the luffing sails. "What's the blasting trouble with those sails? Tighten those lines!"

"There's a problem, Captain," called one of the sailors who stood below the sails, gripping a taut rope in both hands.

"What is it?"

"Not sure, sir. Only that our efforts to keep the sails full on windward keep failing. The winds keep rising and falling. Then they come at us from another angle. Seems like the airslingers keep losing focus, but we've no idea why."

"Not...a lack of focus," the woman positioned below the starboard sail said, her face a knot of effort. "Something's interfering."

The captain's face wrinkled into worry and confusion as he stared behind them at the Outland raider. "What is it?"

"I cannot tell you that," she said. "It's as if the lines keep shifting...like the movement of the waves...or as if an undertow drags at them."

"First the breach of the Net and now this? There is more at work here than a mere Outland raiding party." Captain Jayvel turned back to his crew. "Do your best," he ordered. Then he lowered his voice. "Keep the airslingers working, and send every other gifted or adept aboard to my cabin." He headed for his cabin, his steps full of stern purpose, but his expression tinged with worry.

"Can your crew fight?" Milos asked the Eilaran Second.

"Some few of us have had what training can be had, thanks to Marquon's Protectorate," the officer answered, "but the rest will rely on what skills they have." He gave Milos a small shrug. "I've often given thanks that our airslingers have managed to keep us from a direct battle all the turns I have served aboard the Hawk." He stared across the frothy water at the dark ship on the horizon. "Let's hope that when the sun sets on today's actions our ancestors have our gratitude to receive and not our sorrow to soothe."

Chapter 24

"You act as though I haven't tried." Aertine said in exasperation. She sat back heavily in the chair, head tilted and eyes raised to the sky. "Ancestors keep us. I have used every skill I know. I have tried every stone there is. What you are suggesting cannot be done. The memories were embedded by the hands of those who are beyond us. We cannot undo their works. We have not the skills to do so." She set her jaw.

"But how is it done?" Kira asked. "Not all people are skilled with stones, nor plants, and especially not water. Some, I am told, particularly now, are not skilled at all. Are the memories of only those with skills passed on?"

Aertine gave her a sour look. "Once it was rare for one of the Eilar to be born unskilled. An anomaly to be sure, but even those without skills have value and have something to offer."

"I did not mean to be insensitive," Kira replied. "I merely wish to learn, to understand." She stood and paced as she spoke. "There is so much I do not know. Yet, so much I am expected to do." She sat roughly in her own chair. "I cannot do this alone. I need your help."

Devira raised her brows at her sister.

Aertine glowered at her, blinked, then nodded. She took a sip of her tea before continuing. "Once, all our people were able to leave behind the memories they chose by directly placing them in the keeps. However, because of the…loss of abilities…over time, a process has been created whereby an adept will channel the experience of an unskilled into the memory keep, thereby retaining knowledge of all our ancestors."

Kira gazed into her teacup, swirling the dark liquid within it. "What happens when they become filled?"

"When they become filled?"

"Yes." Kira peered up at her. "What happens to the memories when there is no more room in the…vessels?"

Aertine frowned. "They don't."

"Ever? How is that possible?"

"I have no idea." Aertine's forehead wrinkled as she attempted to work it out.

"What of those who build the memory keeps?"

Aertine let out a short laugh of surprise. "No one has built a new memory keep in my time. There has been no need." The smile fell from her face. "We trace our lineage back as far as we choose by visiting as many places as we need. At least, that is the path of those whose connections have not been severed."

Kira sat silent, absorbing this information. Her face grew chilled as the blood drained from it. She had lost sight of how painful this subject was to the Mistra. "I'm sorry—"

Aertine cut her off with a wave of her hand. "I do not wish to hear your apologies."

"But this destruction of the keep, our, your family's memory keep, it must then touch many others as well."

"Not so many who cared to admit it while Matriarch Kyrina still ruled," Aertine grumbled. "There are those who see nothing wrong with distancing themselves from their family lines."

Devira pursed her lips.

"Besides, the natural distance often becomes greater as we grow older and our offspring make new connections with other families. Choices." Aertine avoided looking at her sister as she continued to speak, but it was clear there was some bitterness between them regarding the subject. "We are created of our choices, even down to choosing which of our lines to trace back and how far." She let out a small derisive laugh. "'Ancestors preserve us.' Such sentiments have become to some mere words repeated in times of wonder or duress. And, yet, there are those of us..." She turned away, leaving the thought unfinished.

Kira sat for a moment, attempting to understand, but it was beyond her how a person could choose which of their lineage to own and which to erase. Finally, she pushed it aside as unimportant, and circled back to the key issue that had snagged her thoughts. "If the memory keeps never fill to overflowing, they can't be simple containers, can they? Not like pitchers or buckets. There has to be something more to it."

"I suppose you may be correct, but if there is," Aertine said, "it is beyond my skill to sculpt."

"You said now that not all are skilled, some memories are...channeled...by adepts into the keeps."

"That is correct."

"How is it done?" Kira asked.

"By making a blood connection."

"A blood connection?" Kira blanched.

"Don't look so appalled," Aertine told her. "We're not savages. It doesn't take much blood for a channeling. Even our Physics, who have sworn to do no harm, are not opposed to participating in a channeling."

"Aertine is correct." Devira raised her teacup to her mouth and blew across the cooling surface. In deep thought, she watched the tiny ripples form and move away from her.

"I do not understand the way of water," she said quietly, setting her teacup down onto the wooden table between them. "But I do understand something about blood. And there are similarities between water and blood."

Aertine shifted forward, an expression of disdain on her face.

"I did not say they were the same," Devira said before Aertine could voice her complaint. "Only that they have similarities. Besides," she continued, "I was going to say that despite that, I still don't understand how one might undo another's skilled work in such a way."

"Which is exactly my point." Aertine glanced at Kira. "It would be much akin to unraveling a tapestry." She gave them a meaningful look, before continuing in a quiet tone, the way one would speak to a child. "One could never reweave the threads in precisely the same order."

I suppose she thinks that I am as much a child as any young Eilar, Kira thought as she stroked Kelmir's velvet ears. Despite her connections with her companions, and the minor techniques her real mother had taught her, she still lacked the most basic Eilaran knowledge and training. Yet, Matriarch Kyrina had bequeathed real power to her. Power she had somehow used to help defeat Kavyn. Why then, did she feel so helpless, now?

Vaith sat contentedly upon the windowsill devouring the cakes Aertine had brought specifically for him. Kira had had to work to keep the grin from her face at Aertine's awkwardness in asking to feed the wyvern. It wasn't merely boys and men who were smitten by the little dragonlet. Perhaps, she thought, they could find more commonality between them with Vaith as a starting point. It would be well if she could develop something akin at least to friendship with her only remaining relatives.

Already, Aertine had become a conspirator in this endeavor, despite her dislike of Kira. Devira had made it clear early on that what she was thinking of doing with

Kavyn's broken sphere would likely draw challenges from the Council should they be discovered. The Council was strict about keeping a close control on what the Eilarans still maintained in the way of skills. With their people's dwindling skills, they had become more and more controlling, worried that any misuse of power might hasten that decline. No risk was to be undertaken in regard to that. Devira was especially definite about them keeping even their discussions of the stone a secret.

Kira agreed. She'd been less than forthcoming to the Council regarding the totality of the events that had played out in the Guardian's chamber. Truth be known, she still had trouble believing what had happened herself. Had she not been there, she wondered what she would think of the story of what had taken place.

Was she lying to herself when she'd determined that the omission of certain details, such as the nature of Kavyn's stone, would benefit not only herself, but everyone around her? She gazed at Devira. She trusted her Physica, but she hadn't even told *her* everything. And, after her long questioning by the Council immediately following the event, she'd not mentioned the matter to anyone again.

Until she'd asked Devira to consider her plan to recreate Kavyn's powerful orb. Devira had balked at first, frightened by the mere thought of being once more in the vicinity of something capable of channeling such power. But Kira had worn her down, at least as far as investigating the stone's capabilities. Her final argument seemed to sway the Physica to her way of thinking. "If we can replicate the making of such a tool, perhaps we can repair the Net," she'd said, and saw Devira's position shift. Protection and care were the keys to this woman's soul. Kira knew it and had used it to unlock her will.

A wisp of guilt wrapped itself around her recollection, but she waved it away like so much errant candle smoke. Whatever the lever, it was worth using. Though Milos and

Marquon had convinced the Council that the Protectorate was needed, could provide security to Eilar, Kira knew better. She had seen first-hand the destruction of war, the death and loss it wrought. So many, including her own parents, had been lost when the Outland raiders had swept across Aestron.

So much bloodshed seemed to cling to her past. Some of which had been directly shed by her. Visions rose up before her; Jolon, Mayet, Toril. She rubbed her palms together as if she could rid herself of the crimson that still seemed to stain her hands.

No. War and the destruction it brought must be kept from these shores by any means possible. And away from the child now growing inside her. If the remaking of Kavyn's stone was the key to unlocking the source and power of the Guardians and the only way to reestablish the protections of Eilar, dangerous or not, this was the path she must pursue. Though Devira had been adamantly against the idea from the start, Kira had found the means to convince her. And she in turn had convinced Aertine. But the Dual Adept had continued to be stymied in sussing out the making of Kavyn's stone. After Varnon's wounding, she'd labeled any further efforts as dangerous and unwarranted and had finally given up any attempt at repairing the stone.

So now, here they all sat, speaking plainly about her latest intentions. Well, arguing about them, actually. Kira had spent the better part of the afternoon explaining to them her reasoning for why it should work. However, she wanted to first test her theory on the family's broken memory stone, and Aertine was having none of it.

"All this talk is for naught. I won't have you finishing what that...what Matriarch Kyrina started, by destroying the last remnants of our family's entrustment," Aertine said again. "I cannot lose that." The last was said in a near whisper, in a voice unusually thick with emotion.

"Not yours alone to lose," Devira chided her. "Nor yours alone to decide." She raised a gnarled hand to cut off Aertine's next explosion. "Though, I agree with you, it is too much to ask." She gave Kira a slight bow of her head. "I beg your understanding of our feelings on this, *Matriarch.*" She fixed her gaze on Aertine as she emphasized Kira's official title.

Kira bit her lip to keep from blurting out that she had as much to lose as they. More, really, as so many of the answers she had come to Eilar seeking remained elusive. Her lineage, her ancestry and all their collective memories, too, lay within the shattered memory keep. But she dared not reveal her true heritage to anyone. Not even her own kin. "I understand you are frightened," she said with more calm and diplomacy than she felt. "But I implore you to consider how much more is at stake. Eilar will not stand against a full assault, when it comes."

Aertine shifted uneasily in her chair. "You mean, if it comes."

"I mean, *when.*" Kira leaned forward, gripping the edge of the table. "We have already been tested. And Kavyn's damage to the land's defenses...I cannot fix that." She heard the desperation in her own voice and sat back in sudden resignation. "It appears, according to you, no one can."

Aertine frowned. "I said we have not the understanding of how they were created, and that none that I know likely have the skill needed. But you?" She held out her hands toward Kira. "You are our Guardian, now. The Pillars remain intact. Why can you not simply reconnect with them as the Matriarch did?"

"Because," Devira answered for her, "it is not so simple as you make it sound. It never has been. The weight of what our Matriarch endured at the hands of the Consort's assassins and the loss of her daughter was not the only thing that twisted her mind."

Aertine gaped at her sister. "You never told me this."

"You had no need to know before. And a person's health, even that of the mind, is a matter kept between physic, or mentalist, and patient. You know this." Devira gestured with a fist folded in to her chest, the Eilar sign of an oath made and kept. "It is something I have reminded you of on more than one occasion." There was more than a hint of annoyance in her tone.

"But I saw what is possible," Aertine shot back. "I sensed her make the connection." She pointed at Kira, then dropped her hand. "The flow of power...She wasn't anywhere near the Guardian's seat. Nor, has she been bound."

Kira shook her head. They had been going round like this for what seemed like turns. "I connected with the energy that lies beneath us, with the paths that flow deep in the earth. But, because of Kavyn, the pillars and the Net have been severed from those paths. I cannot reach them. I cannot even find the linkage, no matter how hard I try." Perhaps, she thought, the fault was not merely with whatever destruction Kavyn had caused, but also with her. After all, she was not truly the Matriarch's heir. Her blood was not of that lineage. Perhaps that was why she had been unable to find the missing paths to the pillars and the island's protective net.

She chewed at that in her mind, wondering again if it would be best to confess the truth. If not to share the information with both of these women, her aunts by blood, or at the very least to offer the burden up to Devira as a secret to be kept by her personal physic. But the Matriarch had set this weight upon her as she had passed on to the wheel, had bequeathed it to her in trust. Had seemed so certain this was the correct path. Did she not have a responsibility to try to make good on that trust? Besides, sharing the secret with Devira would merely serve to place another wedge between her and her lifemate, Zoshia. And Kira could not bring herself to add to the discord between the two.

Mayhap, it was time for her to stop asking for permission to act and begin behaving like a true Matriarch.

"Enough. I asked for your blessing to undertake this trial, because I wish to honor your...our traditions. I desire your permission, but I do not require it." She rose to her feet and faced the two women seated before her. "Our Matriarch Kyrina destroyed your family's memory keep. I wish, not only to find a way to protect this land, but to put things right between our...lines." She strode to the door and opened it, signaling that their discussion was at an end. "But if I need go against your wishes and work alone to fulfill my duty to our people and this land, I will do what I must."

Aertine gaped at her, but Devira rose and crossed the room. "You will do as you see fit." She bowed her head and opened her hands to Kira in a sign of respect before leaving.

"Ever the good servant," Aertine said to her sister's back, shoving her chair out as she stood. "Yes, you may do as you wish," she told Kira, "but I do not have to bow and scrape and pretend to acquiesce." She marched from the room and Kira swung the heavy door shut behind her, then leaned against the sturdy surface to calm herself.

Aertine was so stubborn! It was exhausting to deal with the woman. And as much as Devira had shown deference to her, Kira knew the Physica was as upset by her insistence to go through with her plan as Aertine. She only hoped that neither of them was angry enough to go to the Council and speak against her. Then again, she thought, her defiance rising, she was the Matriarch. What could the Council do? Suddenly exhausted, she sagged against the door. On second thought, perhaps that was a question better left unanswered, at least for the time being.

She shifted her thoughts to the puzzle of the stone and the memory keep. Would it truly be akin to unraveling an intricate weaving? And what if she was unable to retwine the threads of that tapestry? Would it come out distorted, or destroyed completely?

"I know they think it cannot be done," Kira said aloud. "But I know no other way." Her companions sat silent, watching her. "You could at least be supportive," she told them. Vaith let out a low chirrup and went back to preening.

Chapter 25

The day had become overcast as the air adepts continued to struggle with the shifting winds, but still the Outland ship closed in on the Gilded Hawk.

"Bring up the heaviest cargo and toss it off the stern," the captain ordered.

Crewmembers not busy with the steering and shifting of wind and sails leaped to work. Lining up between the hold and the stern of the ship, they passed crates and barrels of goods along the line, dropping them into the water where they splashed into the ship's frothy wake. Milos joined them, taking a place in the line, as did the Aestron sailors, who sweated with both fear and effort. More than once, Milos caught Stronar sneering at him. Milos ignored the brutish sailor and kept to his work. Despite the Aestron sailor's need to target Milos for his blame and anger, they were all in this together now.

With every splash, Milos imagined the lightened ship moving faster over the water, but the Outlander ship continued to gain on them, not once turning aside to try and recover the floating goods that bobbed upon the sea.

Once the last of the cargo had been tossed into the sea, the captain called up his officer. "Either they're not after the cargo, or they think we have something more precious on board." He shook his head. "We'll never outrun them at this pace."

The captain's second, Relten, examined the lowering sky. "It might go hard on the Hawk," he said, "but there may be enough weather to manipulate."

The captain's brow wrinkled with worry, but he hesitated no more than a moment. "Then do it," he ordered.

Relten called out orders and several crewmembers came forward and joined the air adepts. They held out their hands and the wind suddenly dropped. The Outlander ship raced after them while overhead the clouds that had been following gathered together growing dark and ominous. Rain began to fall. First a few icy drops plinked down, then more, turning into a downpour. The wind whipped up again and thunder rumbled. The little sloop's sails billowed outward and the Hawk skidded ahead, once more.

The crew set to work, lashing down the remaining loose items and taking up position for sailing out the storm. The faces of the skilled grew as ashen as the sky, but they continued to work. Behind them, the pursuing ship shrank away, disappearing into the opaque expanse. Those not engaged in the weather-making, cheered.

* * *

Hours later, the way before them cleared. They sailed out of the storm and into a calmer sea. Relief flooded over Milos until the man in the crow's nest called out. "Ships ahead, Captain. Gray sails!"

Milos ran to the prow and stared out at the demoralizing sight before them.

Not a single ship, but more than a half-dozen vessels, large and bulky. Three carried the telltale trappings of barrage ships. Each trebuchet large enough to toss bucketfuls of lethal dragon's fire. They would be manned with enough crew to work their devastating war machines.

The rest of the ships sat low in the water. Marine haulers, likely filled with men and equipment ready for a fight. Or a quick takeover of the Eilaran's homeland. Milos' thoughts roamed back to the years of the Outlander war on Aestron. To Toril and his army. And, finally, to Kira. Life was always a gamble. There were never any guarantees. One turn of the wheel to the next and the game could easily change. At least, they had had a chance to spend those few moons together.

"What do they want?" Dahl asked, his voice raspy with barely restrained fear. "Why can't they just let us go home?"

Milos shook himself loose from his memories. "I doubt they even know we're aboard," he told Dahl. "Most likely they only want the ship and its cargo."

"Then why didn't they take the cargo when the captain threw it overboard?"

"I don't know," Milos told him. "Perhaps, we merely happen to be in the wrong place at the wrong moment."

"Again?" The boy gazed at the ships that sat a short distance off the ship's bow. They waited, like cats preparing to pounce. "And why are there so many of them?"

"That's a good question." Milos searched the ships that would soon surround them, seeking something that might distinguish the Outlanders' flagship. If they could spot it and do something to incapacitate it...But what?

The Eilaran vessel had no real weaponry aside from their few hand weapons. They had always relied on their adepts and skilled crewmembers to keep them out of trouble. Another reason so little trade took place between the island nation and their distant neighbors across the sea.

As they watched, the lookout shouted down to the Gilded Hawk's captain. "Another ship on the horizon, hard astern!"

The Captain was giving more orders, but Milos stood at the rail and watched the pursuing ship come toward them. His stomach soured. If he didn't know better, he'd think the damned thing held an ill will against them.

The Eilaran Second officer stepped up beside him. "The Captain's a good man, but he's not been faced with anything like this before."

"Will he fight?"

"If they choose to board, they'll get a fight, but there's enough of them that it won't much matter. They can board us one at a time once we're full-stopped. It's a mere matter of numbers and time."

Milos ran his knuckles across his chin and nodded in agreement with the Eilaran's assessment. "They'll send a soft crew first to test our resolve. If we don't surrender, and we survive the first assault..."

"They have fire power on their side, if they prefer not to waste men on us."

"Dahl," Milos said, "promise me you'll go below when the time comes."

"But I can help." Dahl stood straight and tall. There was fear in his eyes, but there was also courage.

"It isn't that you can't." Milos shook his head. "Only that I wish you wouldn't. Your captain wouldn't have wanted it, either." He dragged his hand through his hair, feeling the damp of the storm still in it. "Do you understand?"

Dahl squinted up at him, his face serious. "Aye. I understand, but I still think I could help."

"Relten," the Captain said as he passed. "Join me in my cabin."

"Aye, Captain. Listen to your friend, boy." The Eilaran Second patted Dahl's shoulder. "You can help us best by staying alive."

Dahl's face fell and he stared at the deck. "Aye, Sir," he mumbled.

Milos gave the man a grateful look. "Thank you."

"See you on the rising tide." The Eilaran held up his hand, offering Milos the formal sign of respect, then hurried off to catch up to the captain.

Milos stood at the rail and watched the approaching vessel, wondering whether or not the Eilaran would choose to fight.

Chapter 26

The sun lowered in the sky, setting it ablaze with a cascade of pinks and golds. Kira stood beside the broken memory stone. Her hands shook as she surveyed the damage Matriarch Kyrina had caused. The damage Kira had, as of yet, been unable to repair, despite her progress at her lessons, pitiful as it was.

She had her shields up to keep from being once more overwhelmed by the bits and pieces of broken memories that haunted this place. Her first attempt had ended so badly, she'd stayed away for a full two days, nursing her aching head and battered senses. But her need to unravel the mystery of the power stone had driven her back.

She tried not to worry over that first attempt, the threads of memory that had slipped through her fingers like the unraveling of a tapestry. The way the sorrowful emotions connected to the main remembrance had pushed inside her brain and lodged there, roiling and circling like a storm wind that would not let up until she'd been overcome and cried out.

Vaith and Kelmir had been suddenly beside her, pulling

her up and away from the clamor and chaos that slammed inside her head. Somehow, with the help of her companions, she had staggered back to her room in the keep where she had collapsed onto the bed for the remainder of the day. She'd wondered then if Aertine was right, that her attempts were at best a waste of time. Her mind had filled with the possibilities of what they might be at their worst. Yet, she felt compelled to keep trying.

Now that she was here once more, ready to test her latest theory, she was having more second thoughts. What if she failed again? What if, as Aertine feared, all she succeeded in doing was destroying what little remained of her family's legacy? What if, like Matriarch Kyrina, her attempt to control this power drove her mad?

Her loneliness since Milos had gone seemed a weight that pressed her down, forcing her spirits deeper and deeper into a gray place inside her.

Suddenly, she wished she hadn't left Vaith and Kelmir in the Guardian's keep and told them to stay away. After all, they had been her salvation at her last attempt. Yet, she would have enough trouble managing to correctly finesse her shielding to allow in only the specific threads of memory she would be manipulating, without having them close enough to connect with her, all while also shielding the growing life inside her. A life that, though she had not wished for, she would protect with her own.

Her most recent progress in her lessens with Master Amark had inspired her, given her a tentative grasp on the more subtle workings of her skills. The discovery that the way in which she drew upon the power must be matched to the task at hand. Rather than pull upon it as if grasping a handful of wool, she'd learned that by pulling on a single thread, she was able to better control the power, using that strand of power for a single focused task. After numerous tries, she had finally been able to extract additional strands without losing her control on the previous threads.

115

"Well done," Master Amark had praised her. "You've made a leap forward. He'd raised his palm in salute of her accomplishment.

Kira's face warmed at the remembrance. It had still seemed such a tiny step forward compared to what knowledge she still lacked, but it had also made her happy to have finally rewarded the patience of her teacher. And, she thought, this small step might be exactly what she needed for her current work. At least, it had renewed her hope.

She rolled her head on her neck to loosen the tenseness in her shoulders as she'd been taught to do before each lesson, then kneeled down. Before her sat a deep bowl filled with fresh water from the pitcher she had brought with her.

Once the water settled, she picked up a fist-sized chunk of broken stone from the memory keep, cradling it in her hands.

Glancing around to be sure she was alone, hidden from sight by the untended overgrowth, she wished once more she could perform this task somewhere else. But after surveying as many of the memory keeps as possible without arousing suspicion and wandering the length and breadth of the city, she had discovered that certain lines of power crisscrossed exactly where each keep was placed. This placement over the lines of power must be important. *Before experimenting, a good recipe should be followed until one knows the exact combination and order of ingredients.* It was something Brilissa, Tem Hold's cook, had told her on more than one occasion. And Kira felt certain it applied to what she was about to attempt even more than making a good hearty stew.

The reminder of Tem Hold and Milos stabbed at her heart, but she choked away the emotion and focused on her task. Heresta would say, *what ifs are worries that seek attention before their time*, she thought. And all my focus needs to be here and now on this stone.

Still kneeling on the ground, she gripped the stone in her fist until the sharp edge of it cut into her palm. The burning pain helped clear her mind of all other thoughts. As the thin line of blood flowed across the surface of the stone, she thrust her hand into the bowl until both fist and stone were fully submerged. Then, in much the same way Ardea had taught her so many years ago, she pushed her thoughts beneath the water. Once her mind had dipped below the surface, she opened herself up to allow the energy from the lines that flowed beneath the memory keep slowly fill her.

It pulsed, like a throbbing heart, moving through her in time with her pumping blood. A small mental push against the broken piece of stone set off the sound of voices inside her head, causing her to gasp and jerk her mind away in fear. The searing pain of her last failed attempt had sent her tumbling backward, spilling stone and water and blood across the cobbled walkway. She still did not know how much damage she may have incurred on the memory keep with that mishap. A repeat of that failure was not acceptable.

After a moment, she forced herself back to the stone, exerting as fine a level of control as possible, slowly allowing the thoughts to enter her bit by bit, like filtering sediment through a tight-woven sieve; a man's quiet reflection, a baby's gurgle, an elder's sorrow, a woman's joyful remembrance. All these came to her, not merely into her mind, but entered her fully, moving her senses and emotions so that she fully experienced what the original makers of these memories had experienced. Each one burned bright behind her closed lids, becoming separate threads within a woven tapestry. Threads that swam and blurred, slipping in and out of focus, a multitude of murmuring voices and sensations overlaying one another at turns. She struggled to keep them from overwhelming her and distracting her from her purpose.

Focusing on a single memory, she pulled at it, mentally grasping at the slippery end of it. Using her newly developed skills, she brought it into sharper focus, then teased it away from the others until she held only that one. With great care, she opened a place inside her mind, then shifted the memory out of the stone and into herself. Once there, she simply had to hold it intact long enough to let it slip through her, pulsing in time with her heart, to slowly slide out into the water along with the thin trickle of her blood.

By the time the single strand had been extracted, she felt drained, but moving one memory would not be enough to convince Aertine and Devira that what Kira wanted could be accomplished.

She refocused and repeated the process, pulling several more threads from the stone, one by one, and transferring them into the water. Then, while still holding onto the slippery lines of energy, she let go of the rest of the memories, releasing them back into the stone as she drew her hand from the water. Surely, it was merely her imagination that the stone seemed lighter as she set it down beside the bowl.

She sat back on her heels, exhausted and overwhelmed. If this is what it would take to remove only a few memories from the keep, how would she manage to extract them all? And what must be contained in the shards of Kavyn's power stone? The contents would surely be less light and friendly than these ancestral memories.

Not to mention that she hadn't yet moved a single memory to a new vessel. She gazed at the heap of broken rock and thought of all the generations of memories that must be stored there. She leaned over the bowl of pinkish water feeling defeated.

A sudden bout of nausea caused her to turn her head away from the bowl. With shaking hands, she wrapped a cloth around her still oozing wound, pressing the bandaging against the cut to stop the bleeding. She rested beside the bowl until her stomach settled and her breathing grew normal.

She sighed. The task was insurmountable. Especially now that she must move cautiously, to protect the growing life inside her. Yet, she could not stop now.

She strengthened the shields she had woven between her and the child, praying to Troka that her new skills would be enough to both protect the child and complete her work.

She took out the faceted crystal she had brought with her. It glittered in the sunlight, its polished surface casting off rainbow colors. It was much smaller than the chunk of stone, and would likely hold less energy, if indeed there was anything to the idea of a container, after all. But this was simply an experiment and, if it worked, the small crystal would hopefully be temporary.

She dropped the crystal into the water, watching as it settled on the bottom beneath the ripples. She pulled the lines of energy into the bowl, once more gathering the threads together. Recalling her lessons, she gently pushed past the surface of the crystal and interlaced the memories within it. After a few moments, the water lost the pink hue it had held, becoming transparent. Kira gasped and released her grip on lines. The crystalline surface snapped back into place. The stone sat at the bottom of the bowl, inert.

She peered at the crystal, overwhelmed by a rush of worry, and chastised herself at her clumsiness. Had her sudden loss of control ruined the work? There was only one way to know.

Careful to use her undamaged hand, she reached in and grabbed hold of the crystal. She let it rest her trembling palm and opened herself to it. The memories flooded through her. The voices were clear, sounding as if their owners were right beside her. Her exhaustion dropped away, and her eyes grew moist. The memories! The threads she had pulled from the chunk of stone, at least. All of them. They had moved from the rock into the crystal. Broken threads though they were, they now resided in a new place.

She let go of the past, closing herself off to the recollections of her ancestors.

Exhaustion overwhelmed her as she surveyed the wreckage surrounding her. Would she ever be able to transfer all of it? And once that work was done, would she be able to weave the threads together, reconnect the broken strands and render the original memories fully intact? Or would Aertine's shredded tapestry example prove to be correct?

Perhaps. But though it might take a lifetime to restore these ancestral memories, Kira was determined to try. More importantly, however, she might now be able to transfer the energy from Kavyn's shattered stone into another vessel.

If only Aertine could be convinced to help.

The thought both energized and frightened her. What if they managed to replicate his work? What would they discover?

With shaking hands, she emptied the contents of the bowl, saying a prayer of thankfulness to Troka, the Goddess of the wheel, for giving her the opportunity to make things right, to repair the damage that had been done for her sake, not solely for Aertine and Devira, but for all the Eilaran people.

She only wished she could find a way to make things right for Milos, and herself, as well.

Chapter 27

Milos braced himself as the impact of the two ships shuddered through him. The shockwave rippled across beam and spar. The ship's luffing sails shivered against the now cloud-free sky.

He stood with the Eilaran crew, weapons at the ready. Across from him, the Aestrons also prepared to fight, but Stronar gave Milos a glare that told him that if an opening presented itself, he'd as soon gut Milos as any of the Outlanders who were preparing to board the ship.

Large hooks were cast over the rails and the Outlander crew heaved their ship closer. With the grappling hooks in place, dozens of fierce men armed with sharpened blades swung across and thudded onto the deck of the Gilded Hawk.

Their angry battle cries raced before them as they swarmed over the side of the ship. In answer, the Eilaran crew stood quiet, gripping their weapons and saving their energy for the coming fight. From the corner of his eye, Milos saw the Aestron First Mate and most of his followers slip below decks just as the fighting started. Cowards!

Before he could do or say anything, dozens of men crashed together on the schooner's deck. Metal and wood clashed against metal and the fighting began in earnest. The space seemed impossibly small now, filled with so many men swinging their weapons.

A thin man with an angry scar over one eye lunged at Milos, jabbing his heavy blade forward. Milos turned the man's thrust aside easily and cut high across the chest. Blood spilled from the man's wound. He stumbled back, was caught on the side of the head by something heavy and went down. The Eilaran who had swung the stave barely glanced at Milos before repositioning her weapon for another blow. Milos wondered at the courage of the woman to wade into a melee of this sort with no more than a blunt weapon. She was not alone, of course, many of the Gilded Hawk's crew were armed only with clubs and staves.

But he hadn't time to wonder long about it as a fresh assailant came at him. Milos dodged and parried, but his new attacker clearly had plenty of experience with a blade. The two men danced across the deck, dodging one another's blows, while trying to keep clear of the combatants around them. Milos slipped in something foul and the Outlander grinned and pressed his attack. But Milos righted himself and pressed back. Around them rose the sound of men locked in battle, grunting, swearing, occasionally crying out in pain and, too many times, gasping out a final breath. His attacker found an opening, his blade slicing through shirt and jerkin, cutting into flesh. Milos suddenly found himself retreating before the man's increased frenzy, his shoulder crying out with searing agony. He pushed the pain aside, locking it into a deeper place, and focused on staying alive as his attacker continued to press the attack, finally backing him up against the ship's railing.

His opponent grinned in anticipation of finishing his foe, but his overconfidence brought him in close and his eyes gave away his move. Milos caught the man's blade on his own, catching him off balance and causing him to close the distance until he was suddenly near enough Milos could smell the man's sweat.

The Outlander snarled like a feral animal. "Give it up," he said, heaving with exertion. "We've got you outnumbered."

"Outmanned is not outfought," Milos responded between his own rapid gasps.

Beside them, a coil of rope lay on the deck. He swung his body away, pulling his assailant closer to the rail. The man's foot caught in the ropes and he stumbled. Milos slipped behind him and shoved with his good shoulder, sending the man toppling over the rail and into the dark sea with a heavy splash.

"Clever," rasped a voice from behind him.

Milos spun around to find a burly sword-wielding foe closing the distance between them. A trained marine by the looks of him, all muscle and sinew, he slammed his sword downward where it collided with Milos' blade. The strength of the blow rattled Milos to the bone, but he drew back with practiced precision, leaping out of the man's reach. Brute strength would wear him down if he let it, but it would wear down the attacker just as quickly, if the defender could stand his ground long enough. Again the big man attacked. Again, Milos blocked and dodged. Back and forth, their vision narrowing. The rest of the battle fell away as their focus on one another became the only thing that mattered.

Slay or be slain.

The deck beneath their feet had become slick with blood and sweat. The bodies of the slain were now hazardous noncombatants that could take a man down even in death. Milos leaped over the corpse of a man he had earlier seen working the sails of the Hawk, forcing himself to think solely of the fight. There would be time later, as there always was, for the winners to mourn their losses. For the losers, well, if there was any life left in them, they would mourn as well. But now was not the time to be distracted. Milos found his strength flagging before his assailant. Even with all the drilling he had done with the Eilaran Protectorate over the past moons, his opponent's expertise and stamina were proving to be more than a match. He gritted his teeth and doubled his efforts at keeping the larger man at bay, setting his jaw and assuming an air of confidence he no longer felt. Sweat dripped into his eyes and his worn boots slipped more than once on the blood-slicked deck.

Suddenly, a voice rang out over the din. "Surrender, or I kill your Captain and every skilled adept on this ship."

The Outlander Milos was fighting grunted in frustration and slowed his attack long enough to flick his eyes toward the voice. A tall man with red-blond hair stood at the helm, though he seemed to hunch forward like an old man, his hand gripped a blade that he pressed against Captain Jayvel's throat. "Look around you. My ships merely await my order to close and add their fighting men to the fray. You are outnumbered." He yanked the Captain's head up, stretching his throat like an animal being prepared for slaughter. "You will lose." He waved his knife over the heads of the captives at his feet.

Most of the skilled Eilaran crewmembers; the airslingers and weather weavers, the menders, even the ship's Physic, were among the captured. They all kneeled on the deck, their heads lolling as if they'd been knocked senseless. Arrayed behind them were a group of Outlanders and the Aestron sailors, behaving far too friendly with one another.

Filthy traitors, Milos thought, standing down, but keeping his blade at the ready, and wondering where the rotten Aestron First Mate, Stronar, was lurking. Probably down in the bilges with the other rats.

The hunched man leaned closer and said something low in the Captain's ear.

Captain Jayvel shook his head.

"That one," the man said, jerking his chin at one of the ship's airslingers.

An Outlander stepped forward, yanked the half-conscious Eilaran up to his feet and unsheathed a wicked looking blade. The airslinger wobbled, but made no move to escape or defend himself.

Captain Jayvel's face hardened. "Do as he says," he said, finally.

The Outlander's leader grinned in triumph as the fighting ground to a halt.

Milos hated to give up, but he understood the Captain's need to protect his people. He knew from what Marquon had told him, what the loss of skilled men and woman would mean, not only to them, to this crew, but all of the Eilaran people. The ship's crew would sacrifice whatever was necessary to keep their skilled alive, especially their adepts.

Suddenly, the attraction of being so mentally abled dimmed. Milos would hate being a liability. Though, truth be told, the Eilaran were learning to fight in other ways. He thought Marquon, Tesalin and the other members of the Eilaran Protectorate he had trained with. Their fighting skills would have come in handy this day.

Once the sounds of battle had fully faded, the moans of the wounded could be heard.

"That's better," the tall man said, still menacing the captain with his blade. "Now, put down your weapons."

One by one, the Eilaran crewmembers dropped their weapons. The woman with the stave gave a disgusted grunt as she slammed her weapon onto the deck with a resounding clatter. Outlanders surrounded the Eilaran.

Milos leaned forward and set his blade on the deck at his feet, his chest heaving and his wounded shoulder searing. The big man Milos had been fighting sneered. "Too bad. I'd have enjoyed finishing you. Especially after that sneak move you played on Belar. Good thing I hated that lump." He shoved Milos toward the bow where the rest of the Eilaran crew were being herded.

Milos cradled his wounded arm, attempting to lessen the pain of his open wound, which continued to bleed. Now that the fight was over, and his senses took hold, each and every injury made itself known and his body shook with the release of tension. He took a moment to assess the aftermath of the fighting. The Eilaran crewmembers who stood near him glared in the direction of the Outlanders' leader, wearing more than the usual hatred and fury of defeat.

Milos scanned the deck, counting wounded and survivors and searching for Dahl, hoping the boy had managed to stay out of the fighting. There were too few Eilaran standing on the bow and no sign of the boy. Milos forced himself to search the dead and wounded. None of the bodies were Dahl's. Milos breathed a sigh of relief. Until he heard a commotion near the ship's forward hatch.

Stronar had Dahl by the shirt and was dragging him up the ladder. "Caught this one trying to hide." He tossed Dahl onto the deck like a sack of grain.

"Put him with the others," the tall man told him.

Dahl glanced up at Milos, a look of rebelliousness on his face and a trickle of blood running down the side of his head.

Milo forced himself not to show his concern as Stronar kicked and shoved the boy toward the rest of the prisoners. It wouldn't do to remind the brute how much Dahl meant to Milos. At least, not unless he forced Milos to act.

Dahl stumbled as the big man gave him a final kick and sent him sprawling into the legs of the Eilaran sailors.

"Not so important now, are ya?" Stronar said, his lip curling.

As if to negate the man's assessment, pale hands reached for Dahl, helping him to his feet, where he could stand among the Eilaran. Dahl squared his shoulders and started forward. Milos tensed, preparing to move between the boy and Stronar, but before he could intercede, one of the Eilaran placed a firm hand on Dahl's shoulder and gave Milos a nod.

Dahl pressed his lips together. Keeping his mouth shut tight, he glared at his old shipmates with a dark hatred.

Chapter 28

Zoshia sat in silence, dreading what would come next. Though Kira had agreed to assume her place as the Eilaran Matriarch, she continued to find ways to delay and had persistently refused to commit to perform the binding ritual. The Councillors had grown restless and impatient. Their meetings grew more and more anger-filled and divisive. Now, Meryk had called them together to make a determination.

"I call for removal," said Councillor Teldin.

"Removal from what?" Kersin asked. "She has taken on the position of Matriarch in name only. Despite her promise, she continues to make excuses to push back the Binding ritual. She sits upon the Guardian's Seat rarely and with no real intent."

"Then how do we proceed?" Teldin demanded.

"Has anything like this happened before?"

"I have searched the archives and in all our written history, there has never been a Guardian who did not perform the Binding and accept the responsibilities of their position." Councillor Vaspel's fingertips rested on the recording stone that would document their discussion and be stored in the archivist's library.

"What can be done?"

"There are sanctions that can be imposed."

Zoshia slapped her hand onto the table. "Would you truly attempt to impose sanctions on the Matriarch?"

"Why not?" asked Marsal.

"First off, it is unprecedented," Zoshia retorted.

"So was the attack on our shores!" Teldin shouted.

"Perhaps, not in recent times," she answered, "but this island has survived attacks from outside our borders in the past. And it is not as if the attack was guided by her hand."

"There have been other reasons to sanction a ruler," Councillor Kendryn said in a whispery voice. "And how do we know she was not complicit? We have only her word on what took place in the Guardian's Chamber, and it seems a thin story."

Zoshia was glad Devira was not here to listen to this discussion. Her lifemate had been angry enough over the simple request to intervene on the Council's behalf. What would she think of a call for sanctions and, worse, removal? Perhaps, if she spoke convincingly, she might sway them away from this course. "Past rulers have only been sanctioned in the case of truly terrible behavior," she reminded them. "For crimes committed against others, acts that have caused direct harm. Not for mere recalcitrance."

"What you refer to as 'mere recalcitrance' exposes Eilar to real harm, and not merely to a single individual, but to all of us." Marsal waved her arms to encompass everyone at the table. "And all of Eilar. Is that not criminal?"

Zoshia's certainty wavered, but she pushed forward. "Eilar's survival has never been accomplished by turning against its own rulers. Especially not in a battle of power and will."

"For the past twine of seasons, *we* have been its rulers," a quiet voice said.

Startled, Zoshia gaped at the Council First.

Meryk shook his head at her, in much the way a scolding parent might an errant child. Then he plowed ahead. "While Kyrina sat upon the Guardian's seat, it was the Council that ruled," he reminded them. "Even our new Matriarch has admitted as much in handing over so much of the day-to-day responsibilities of governance. This Council must lead. Has it not before fallen to us to step in and rule where others cannot? How is that different than now, when our ruler will not?"

"But that is treason—"

He cut off Zoshia's words with a chopping motion. "We have given her ample opportunity to accept her role. What good is a ruler who will not rule? A Guardian who will not guard?" His face grew unreadable, but his voice grew stronger with the passion of his cause. "It is not treason to guide where there is no guidance, to assert the authority that has been refused by the one to whom it falls."

Zoshia's scalp tingled with prickling fear. "What will this mean for us as a people?" she asked, in a quiet voice. "What will this mean for Eilar?"

No one seemed to hear her. They had already moved on to planning their strategy. Their words buzzed in her ears as her thoughts tried to reform in some semblance of logic. She could not sit idly by while this Council sought the usurpation of their true ruler. Every fiber of her knew this. Why did the rest of them not see how they would be destroying their way of life, the very traditions they were sworn to protect? Her muscles twitched and she began to rise in protest, but she gazed around at the earnest faces of her colleagues and saw not greed, nor hunger for power, but fear and a need to survive. To survive and to save themselves and their loved ones. To save their land and their people.

She thought of Devira and her heart seemed to shatter inside her chest. This would be the last straw between them, but what other way was there to save their land, their people, and the life of her one and only love? She sank back down into her seat in despair as their words finally filtered into her brain.

While the current line had not been broken for so many generations, there had been a time in the land's history when an heir had not been produced and rulership had had to be shifted. Perhaps, there was still one among their people who might be skill-born with enough power to begin a new line.

Perhaps, this was for the best. Kira's reluctance to rule seemed to run deep. Was it deep enough that she could be persuaded to step aside without formal action? What they were proposing went against everything many of them had stood for and their long-held beliefs, yet they discussed it as if it were a matter of normal business. And here she was, sitting among them, unable to stop their forward momentum. If nothing else, perhaps she might soften the approach, though Devira might never forgive her. She braced herself before holding up her hand to speak. "It would be better, I think, for everyone, if the Matriarch's heir could simply be persuaded to relinquish her claim. A quiet transference of power."

The First wrinkled his face in contemplation. "And how would we accomplish such a thing? There is no other heir."

"There is at least one adept among the younglings who has a degree of skill likened to our key adepts of the past. The potential start of a new bloodline." She paused a moment to let the idea sink in, well aware that her next words would give them pause. "The boy the Aestron saved may have enough skilled blood to be a viable replacement for our reluctant ruler."

There was an audible gasp from the assembly.

"A boy? But..."

Zoshia held up her hand. "The irony is not lost on me that not only was this boy saved by the man who refused the position of Consort with our current Matriarch, but that the single reason we did not replace our mad...forgive me, our previous Matriarch with her own son was because of his gender." She sighed. What pain and trouble might they have avoided by grooming Kavyn properly, rather than allowing Teraxin to feed his corruption? But that was now the past and they must focus on their future. "But at this juncture, what other path lies open to us? After all, the boy is skilled and, unlike the Matriarch's heir, has been properly trained in the use of those skills, as well as all our ways."

A few of the Councilors nodded in agreement, but Teldin quickly spoke out. "I don't see how this boy could possibly manage the Guardian's seat. Is he not a mere physic adept?"

Zoshia jumped to the defense, quick to maintain the hold she had managed to grasp on a few of the more open-minded of her peers. "It is true he is merely adept in the healing arts, but is our land not in need of healing?"

There was silence in the room as the Councilors considered her words. Finally, all eyes settled on the First.

The old man was clearly unnerved by the suggestion. He chewed his tongue in thought before asking, "What do you propose?"

Zoshia took a deep breath, then plunged forward. "Let us at least agree to have the boy tested. If he can meet the basic challenges, then with the Council's blessing, I will meet with the Matriarch and offer her the opportunity to accede to the Council's request of transference without formal action." She hoped against hope that this time Devira would understand the necessity of helping her persuade Kira to do the right thing. If not...

"If she does not accede," the First said, as if reading her thoughts, "we will convene a Unification and force the transference. Either way, we will have a seated ruler, who can be properly bound as the Eilaran Guardian."

Chapter 29

"That one has value." Stronar spat at Milos. Two Outland marines held Milos roughly by his arms, his hands and feet bound like the Eilaran crewmembers.

"How so?" demanded the Outlanders' leader.

"He and that witch, the one what rules the Eilars, now. They sailed together before she rose up. They're a matched item, if you catch my meaning." Stronar leered at Milos.

"Is that true?" The big blond man asked, eyes intent with interest. "Are you worth keeping alive?"

Milos clamped his jaw shut and glared at the deck in silence.

"Look at me," the man ordered.

One of the marines grabbed Milos by the hair, forcing his head back so their commander could peer into his bruised and swollen face.

"Yaran, convince him." The commander shuffled back and waved at Milos, and one of the Outlander marines punched him in the side, just below his ribs.

Milos sucked in air and ground his teeth to keep from making a sound.

The blond man leaned forward. "Answer me," he demanded from behind clenched teeth.

"He's lying to you," Milos huffed out, trying to catch his breath. "I'm worth about as much as that worthless bilge-drinker." He spat in the direction of the Stronar, who roared and lunged at Milos, struggling to reach him as more of the Outland marines held him back.

"Shut up!" The commander eyed the mate suspiciously, then rounded on Milos. "And why would he go to the trouble of making up a story like that?"

"He's my friend," Milos said, giving the mate a wry smile. "He's trying to save my life by making you think I'm more valuable than I am."

"The blazes, I am," roared Stronar. "Ask the rest of the crew." He gave Milos a filthy look and grinned wickedly. "Better yet, ask the boy."

The Outlander's gaze swept over Milos to the mate and back again, measuring them with a keen eye. "Bring the boy to me."

Milos stiffened as one of the other raiders dragged Dahl across the deck and shoved him to his knees before their leader.

"So, boy. What's your name?"

Dahl glanced at Milos, who kept his face blank. Only the barest twitch of his brow communicating the boy should comply.

Dahl pushed himself up and stood tall, though his hands shook. "Dahl."

"And how is it you came to be in the company of these men?"

"We're shipmates, bound for home is all." Dahl raised his head to look directly up at the Outlander who questioned him, attempting to hide the shiver of fear that cracked his voice.

"And why is it you are sailing on one of the Eilaran vessels?" The big man waved at the ship around him.

"Our ship was wrecked by a storm when we approached their land. We're working our passage home."

"And this one?" He pointed to Milos.

Dahl glanced over and Milos twitched his head, hoping Dahl would not admit to their friendship.

"A passenger." Dahl shrugged. "Some kind of farmer, I think."

"I see." The Outlander reached out and grabbed Dahl's face in his meaty hand and drew his face to his. His ice blue eyes filled with something beyond hate.

Tears formed in the corners of Dahl's eyes, and a whimper escaped him.

"Try again." The man released him. "Even with those worn boots, he's no farmer."

Red marks showed on Dahl's face where the man had held him. Marks that appeared more like burns than bruises.

"I already told you," Stronar growled, "he's—"

"Shut him up," the Outland leader ordered. A big brute stepped forward and punched the mate on the top of his head, toppling him to the deck in a heap.

Milos kept his face clear of the satisfaction he felt at Stronar's treatment. It was a universal truth, seemingly known to all but those who deem it profitable to switch sides: *Once a traitor, always a traitor. And traitors can't be trusted.*

It seemed the same rule applied to instant allies.

"I don't know anything about boots," Dahl said, gingerly touching the red places on his face. "Far as I know, he's only some farmer who needed passage to Aestron."

"Fine," said the Outlander. He jerked his chin at the big man who had clubbed Stronar unconscious. The marine grabbed Dahl roughly by the neck and the back of his shirt. "Toss him overboard." Dahl kicked and struggled as the burly man lifted the boy off his feet. "Sharks are plentiful in these waters, and always ravenous."

"Stop," Milos said, attempting to pull away from his captors. The beefy arms that held him in place tightened on his wounded shoulder and he winced. "Leave the boy alone and unharmed, and I'll tell you what you want to know."

"No!" Dahl cried out.

The Commander waved a hand and Dahl was dumped back onto the deck, where he landed in a heap, struggling to regain his feet.

"I was—*am* a Holder in Aestron." Milos spoke quickly, hoping he could convince the raiders to pass the Eilaran island by and take them all to Aestron. The Eilars were not his people, but at least the Aestrons, who had driven the Outlanders from their shores once before, were better equipped to fight. Besides, given time, he hoped he might come up with a better plan.

Guilt wrapped its coils around him at the thought of bringing these men to his homeland, but a part of him hoped the Outlanders might not actually attack based on their not too distant defeat. Perhaps, they wouldn't know of Toril's untimely death and the recent breaking up of the islands' mercenary army. He thought of Kira and her time with Toril and anger suffused him. He let it simmer along with all of his other ire. He'd let it build to a boil and use it. "I'm worth a fine ransom in my land."

"How fine?" The Outlander eyed Milos's worn boots and Eilaran clothes.

"Fine enough to make it worth your while to keep us all alive until we reach my homeland." Milos locked eyes with the man. "Bring us safely to Aestron, and I'll see that you're handsomely paid for your trouble."

Their leader shook his head. "I'm not inclined to feed and house you and all these others for two moons or more. Nor do I need your pitiful ransom. I have more important business to attend to." He stared across the water in the direction of Eilar.

"Once we make landfall at Aestron," Milos said loud

enough for all the men to hear, "I can make you all wealthy."

The Outlander crewmen grinned, their eyes lighting with greed.

Their leader laughed. "It's a nice story, and possibly even true. But I think you're worth more as the Matriarch's Consort than some simple Aestron Holder." His gaze took on a faraway look. As if he were seeing something no one else could. "Besides, I've got a promise to keep."

Chapter 30

"I have something to show you." Kira held out the crystal.

Aertine glared at her. "What have you done?"

"Here. Take it."

Aertine folded her arms in refusal.

Haltingly, Devira extended her hand, and allowed Kira to place the crystal onto her palm. She gasped and brought the crystal closer, peering at it in wonder. "How?"

Aertine's jaw tightened. "It isn't possible."

"But the proof is here before you," Kira said. "If you would simply open your mind to see what is possible."

"Aertine. Sister." Devira offered the stone to Aertine. "Only try."

Aertine scowled, but she took the stone. Her eyes went wide when she touched it. Then her scowl returned. "It is merely broken bits. Yes, you have managed a transfer, which is a feat I could not manage. But to what end? You may as well have left these threads within the broken stones where they already were. At least they would still be where they belonged." She dropped the crystal onto the table in disgust. "Instead, you have defiled our family's Memory Keep."

"But don't you see?" Kira exclaimed. "This is merely the first step in restoring the memory stone." She picked up the crystal and held it out so it caught the light breaking it into prismatic stars that bounced and glittered across the walls. "And if we can transfer these memories, we can transfer the contents of the broken power stone into a new one."

"No." Zoshia strode into the room. "The Council will never approve. We have no idea what power that stone contained, nor what reproducing it might do. Kavyn's meddling has already crippled our defenses beyond repair." She turned to Devira in anger. "Is this what you have been about? Why you have been so secretive? Slipping away at all hours. I knew you had not fully resumed your Physic's duties. I thought it was merely that you were not yet healed from your fall. But this? This is wrong and you know it. It will never be sanctioned."

"I was not hiding it from you," Devira said. "You simply chose not to see what was before your eyes."

A stunned expression crossed Zoshia's face, quickly replaced by a hard anger. "Do not speak to me so in front of others."

Devira reddened. She set her jaw. "My apologies, Councillor," she said with a frosty edge.

Kira gripped the stone in her hand, hating that she had been the cause of yet more conflict, and angrier still at the uninvited interruption. Aware that she must learn to navigate the politics of this land, she schooled herself before responding. "Please, do not be angry with Devira. As my Physica, she was merely keeping my confidence."

Zoshia frowned at her. "Your confidence is no longer kept, and as a member of the Eilaran Council, I insist that you stop toying with powers of which you have little to no understanding."

Kira stood and faced the Council Second, her own anger rising to the fore. "You do not know what I understand. Unless you've found another way other than an official interrogation to pry into my thoughts."

Zoshia's eyes narrowed. "You dare accuse me?" Her voice had lowered to a deadly growl like distant thunder.

Kira stepped forward, prepared to do battle, but Devira touched her scarred fingers to her wrist. Startled at the level of rage that had risen up at Zoshia's words, Kira let the anger drain from her. She dipped her chin and took in a slow breath. "Thank you," she murmured.

The Physica bowed her head and backed away.

"We need to protect our shores." Kira said after containing her ire. "My efforts—"

"We *need* a Matriarch, one who will assume her duties and her place upon the Guardian's Seat," Zoshia cut her off.

"The Guardian's Pillars are broken, the tools of the Matriarch corrupted." Kira crossed her arms. She knew it would be perceived as the closing off of dialogue, but she didn't care. "You did not see what I saw. You do not know..."

"Are you admitting that you have been less than forthright with the Council? That you have kept from them information that could help our land and our people? Please, tell me more about this treasonous behavior. What else do we not know about you?"

A shiver ran across Kira's skin. "Against whom might the Eilaran's Matriarch commit treason? Herself?"

"You know little of us as a people and even less of our laws," Zoshia told her. "You do not want to test the Council on such a matter."

Kira's head buzzed with alarm. She sensed more than a warning in Zoshia's words. "What does the Council intend?" she asked. "How far have they already moved against me?"

Zoshia's face paled. "The Council works only for the good of Eilar and its people. The power of the Matriarch must be used for the right purpose."

"Used. An apt word. Yes, I saw how Matriarch Kyrina was used." Kira kept her voice low, but the anger that had risen inside her made itself heard. "And how should we trust the Council to know what is right? This Council has not shown such great wisdom in the past." She picked up the glittering stone from the table and allowed the voices of her ancestors within it to buzz against her mind. "I did not ask to be placed in this position. I never wanted to become a ruler. But I will not run from the responsibility that was bequeathed to me. I remain here in order to protect Eilar. You simply need to turn your attention elsewhere and allow me the chance to do so in my own way."

Zoshia glanced at Devira, then looked back at Kira.

Kira locked eyes with her. "I can do this."

"No," Zoshia said. "You cannot."

Kira stared at the Second in defiance, while across the room, Kelmir roused himself from his recent slumber and cocked his ears in the direction of the two women. "Do you forget whom you address?"

Zoshia stood tall. "Do you?"

"I believe I have shown that I do not require the Council's blessing to do as I see fit." Kira clenched the stone in her fist.

"You may have managed to best the Interrogators, but we both know there was no finesse behind the power you used to do so, and they were unprepared. The power the Council can bring to bear is enough to contain even a capable Matriarch, as your mother might attest were she still alive." Pain washed across Zoshia's face, but her words were edged with steel.

"You have no idea what I am capable of." Kira told her. "Nor what my mother might attest to." Perched on the back of Kira's chair, Vaith fluttered his leathery wings nervously.

"Please, stop." Devira interjected herself between them. "I'm certain our Matriarch meant no harm by her suggestion." The touch she laid upon Kira's arm was soft, yet imploring.

Kira did not look away from Zoshia, continuing to hold the Second's eyes with her own.

"Nor did the Council Second intend any disrespect." The Physica's words were clipped, imperative. "Please, forgive her. She speaks on behalf of a Council, and a people, too long without a whole and rational leader." She gave her lifemate a knowing look.

Aertine raised an eyebrow at her sister, the hint of a smile quirking up the side of her mouth at the sudden audacity of Devira's behavior.

Zoshia appeared startled. She gaped at Devira, then stepped back and made a gesture of respect to Kira. "I'm sorry." She shook her head. "The Council has already decided. I am merely the messenger."

Devira gripped her lifemate's hand. "What, Zoshia? What have they decided?"

Zoshia raised Devira's hand to her lips and kissed her scarred fingers. "I'm sorry, my love." She let go of Devira's hand and turned back to Kira. "If you do not proceed with the binding, or choose to step aside. They intend to formally remove you as Matriarch, by any necessary means."

Aertine sat forward, worry darkening her face.

"What does that mean?" Kira tensed. Across the room Kelmir growled low, his ears folding back, and Vaith hissed, preparing to launch himself from his perch.

A shudder ran through Kira as she sent calming thoughts to both of her companions, surprised by their rapid reactions to her emotions. Was their connection growing stronger? Her shielding weaker? Or, with all that had befallen her, was she perhaps already losing her grip as had Matriarch Kyrina before her? Could it be that it was not the bloodline that held power, but rather provided a protection, something that normally gave the Matriarch's heirs the ability to remain sane while being connected to and wielding the power of the land? What then was the true purpose of the Guardian's seat. And what of the Chains of Office?

"It means they will come against you as one, if need be." Devira gave Zoshia an angry look.

"How can they do this?" Kira asked.

"They are the Eilaran Council," Devira told her. "Do not think they hold no power," she warned, refusing to look at her lifemate.

"They will form a full Unification," Zoshia told her. "They will use their entire might against you. The Interrogation you experienced was but a taste."

"They will break you." Devira's voice shook, her meaning painfully clear. "Mentally *and* physically."

The child. Kira's mind raced. Would she truly be able to hold off the entire Eilaran Council, should they decide to beset her? Could she stand up to the threat that they might pose? Could her child?

She glanced at the Council Second and in that moment came to a decision. She would need to play a longer game, to continue her work with the memory stone, but her true intent would need to be hidden. For now, she must give way.

"My apologies," she said to Zoshia, gesturing in deference to the woman's status. "I have not been myself these past days. Please, forgive my...poor manners. And my rash thinking." She settled herself back into her chair, reaching up to stroke Vaith's scaly neck with her fingertips. "I understand the Council's concerns. Perhaps some powers were meant to be left...untested."

Zoshia opened her hands in acceptance. "A wise determination." The Council Second appeared mollified, but Aertine cocked an eyebrow at Kira.

"But," Kira continued, "I still wish to continue to repair the damage done by my...my predecessor, I wish to continue making repairs to the Kystrell family's Memory Keep." She set the stone onto the table and waved her hand over it.

Aertine opened her mouth to speak, but at a glance from her sister, froze.

Zoshia eyed Kira thoughtfully before glancing over at Devira, who averted her eyes. "I shall make your wishes known to the Council. We will provide our...guidance on the matter."

"And I have reconsidered the Council's request to properly take up my... position," Kira continued. "After all, we should be working together as our purposes to ensure the safety of Eilar and all of its people are so aligned. I will perform the binding. She shuddered inwardly before continuing. "I will take my place upon the Guardian's Seat, assuming fully the mantle of Matriarch and the Chains of Office. As soon as the ritual can be arranged."

Devira gaped at her in surprise.

"I will deliver your message to the Council," Zoshia sputtered, seemingly startled at the twist of the conversation and Kira's sudden concession. "I am sure the Councilors will be glad to hear it," she said, but her words sounded unconvincing.

"I'm happy to know I can bring gladness to the Councilors," Kira said, the muscles of her face clenching as she forced a smile.

Devira leaned over the table and reached for the carafe of cooled tisane.

Aertine huffed out her breath as if preparing to speak out against Kira's intentions, but Devira bumped her with her elbow as she refilled her sister's cup. Aertine gave her sister a hard look, then picked up her freshly filled cup, leaned back in her seat and glared at the gemstone that sat on the table before them.

No matter, Kira thought. She would keep working, with or without the Council's approval. The work on the Memory Keep would cover her true efforts. And she would leave Aertine and Devira out of it. They did not need to be involved. Aertine was clearly against the idea, though Kira now wondered what Devira's current thoughts on the matter might be. Not that it would make any difference. The broken power stone was the key to understanding what was coming and be prepared for it. If the Council would not grant her their blessing, so be it. She would protect these people with or without their consent.

And if the binding ritual had been the final strand that had caused Kyrina's madness? She pushed the thought to the back of her mind and focused on the task at hand, to convince Zoshia, and thus the entire Eilaran Council, that their decision to remove her had finally been the push she needed to accept their demands and her role as Matriarch with all the trappings that went with it, and that she would become the tool they expected her to be.

Perhaps, without the interference Kyrina had been subjected to by Kavyn, Kira would survive the role with her faculties intact.

Chapter 31

The Outland leader and a detachment of men remained aboard the captured sloop. It seemed that all of the seafaring Outlanders were Marines, every one of them trained both as warrior and seafarer. A rare combination of talents to an Aestron, but apparently common for the aggressive Outlanders. No wonder they'd managed to attack Aestron in such great numbers, Milos thought. The entire contingency had been able to navigate rapidly across the sea and then leap ashore leaving a bare minimum of men aboard to protect the fleet.

The Outlanders separated the Eilaran adepts and skilled from the rest of the crew before shoving them into the hold. Milos watched, wondering how they managed to tell the difference.

One of the Eilaran sailors noticed his puzzled expression. "It's Ekzarn." She flicked her eyes at the main deck where the Outlander leader stood, feet spread wide, a satisfied smirk on his face. "He's of Eilaran stock. An outcast." She glanced around. "Shalen thinks it's—" A shove from behind cut off the woman's words. They were herded farther down the hold where they were locked into makeshift cells. Milos was relieved when he and Dahl were shoved together into a small metal cage that had been hauled aboard the Hawk and shoved against the curved bulkhead in the ship's storage hold.

"How are you faring?" he asked the boy, as he took stock of the metal bars that surrounded them on three sides.

Dahl didn't speak, but his eyes followed their jailers, watching their backs as they left the captives and headed back above decks.

Concerned by the boy's silence, Milos went down on one knee where he could better look the boy in the eye. "I can't tell you there is nothing to fear," he said, giving Dahl his honesty. "But I can tell you that I'll do everything possible to keep us safe."

Dahl frowned. "First Mate Stronar caught me before I could get hold of the cleaver."

"Lucky for Stronar." Milos used his sleeve to dab at a bloody cut on Dahl's cheek.

Around them, the Eilaran whispered in the shadows. Milos wished once more for the ability to mindspeak as some of their skilled could do.

Chapter 32

Kira tossed and turned, trying to find a comfortable position for sleeping, but the bed was at turns too soft and too hard, too hot and too cold. She threw aside the covers and sat on the edge of the bed, pushing her toes into the soft pile of the carpeting. From the end of the bed, two pairs of eyes glowed in the low light cast by the banked coals glittering in the hearth.

Of course, her restlessness was affecting both Vaith and Kelmir. The big cat especially. After all, he was naturally nocturnal. Kira shivered at Kelmir's anticipation of running in the night. Sensing her echoing need, he leaped from the foot of the bed.

Kira padded on bare feet to the door of the chamber and lifted the latch. The hallway would be empty at this hour, and the doors to the keep would be shut. But the night watchers knew to keep an eye out for Kelmir and would open the way for the big cat. They had grown accustomed to his prowling, unlike some of the more timid staff who stood still as statues when he passed them in the wide hallways.

She swung open the heavy door. *Go, Kel.*

He moved through the keep, silent and swift, heading for the main door. The night watcher started when Kelmir approached, then with quick motions opened the door onto the crisp darkness of early morning.

Cold seeped through the pads of Kelmir's feet as he trotted out through the garden and headed for the path beside the river where he could run freely. Foliage rushed by as he stretched out his gait. He twitched his ears and increased his pace, racing through the chill night.

The path wound along the water's edge, twisting between the clusters of trees.

Up in her chamber, Kira sat before the fire reveling in the feel of the night, the rush of wind, the heady morning scents that filled their brains. Kelmir's sense of freedom, his hunter's alert intensity rushed through her more pronounced than she'd ever known. She let herself slip further into his mind, losing track of where her own body ended and where Kelmir's began. The physical distance between them disappeared as her consciousness settled into place alongside his. Comforting calm enveloped her. Something as near to peace as her new life allowed washed through her.

Muscles bunched and stretched, blood coursed in rhythm with their pounding heartbeat. Slowly, she drifted into a place she'd never been, reveled in the unbounded expanse. A velvet darkness rubbed up against her, lulling her.

Suddenly, a hand reached out, clutching her fingers. "There you are." The silky voice was oddly familiar. "I've been searching for you, everywhere."

She sensed herself slipping away from Kelmir, being drawn elsewhere. A buffeting wave caught her up, and an undercurrent tugged at her. The velvet turned icy and ran cold claws up her spine. Where was she? Where was Kel? Vaith? She reached for them, but on every side there was

149

nothing but the dark void and the voice that tried to compel her. "It will go easier, if you relax and let me in."

Kira flailed in the heavy darkness that surrounded her and gripped her. It pounded against her, weighing her down beneath the heavy velvet curtain that both attracted and repulsed her.

"What's this?" The question was one of surprise. Something reached out for her, stabbing at her midsection.

Pain struck her and radiated from her center. She felt another pull, but the velvet drape contained her. She kicked and clawed at the amorphous walls that imprisoned her.

"No matter. This line will end." The words were dismissive, doubt-tinged, but filled with a fiery need for destruction. The stabbing came again, this time the hate behind it struck her as a physical blow and caused bile to rise into her throat, gagging her.

With a sudden rush of anger, she wrapped her arms protectively around herself and raised her head up out of the suffocating darkness that encompassed her. With great effort, she heaved shut her shields, slamming herself off. A great slash of energy ripped across her thoughts, rending her conscious mind and ripping her away from herself and everything else she'd ever been connected to. Everything, except the small flame of life that flickered inside her.

The darkness subsided. She blinked, trying to orient herself. She lay on her side, her face mashed into the soft rug. Her damp bedclothes clung to her and she shivered. The red glow of coals flickered in the hearth before her, and Vaith chirruped in relief from the mantle, as she rolled over and sucked in precious air.

Outside the chamber door, Kelmir paced in agitation, but she hadn't the strength yet to get up and cross the room to let him in. Nor did she feel able to lift her shields, to open herself up to anything, including her companions, with that dangerous darkness lurking.

She tried to examine what it might be, turning it over

in her thoughts in order to understand it. But her mind recoiled from it. The recollection of what had happened roiled and filled her head with dim, uncertain shadows. Already it grew hazy, as if it had been nothing but a bad dream. But Kira was certain it had been more than that. Something lurked out there in the world. Something dangerous. Something that had attempted to trap her outside of herself. Something, or someone, that hated her, wished to destroy her. And all of Eilar.

Chapter 33

Milos studied his surroundings through half-closed eyes. Beside him Dahl slept fitfully, his thin body wracked with exhaustion. Above them, the Outlander crew was having sport. Probably at the expense of one of the Eilarans. They kept most of the Eilar crew locked up nearby. Milos suspected the Outlanders were drugging their water as they seemed sluggish and confused most of the time. Clearly, the Outlanders knew the Eilarans might have some skills they would be able to use against them, despite the current decline of their gifts, if given the chance.

Once more, Milos found himself wondering about it. His friend Marquon had not spoken freely of the issue and Milos had learned not to ask. It was as if the Eilaran people were ashamed of their loss. Indeed, as Milos had learned in his time on the island, the Council had for years preferred to remain ignorant of the situation, rather than take any action to guard against the potential threats to which it exposed them. At least, that was how Marquon had bitterly described their behavior. "Our children continue to die, our skills vanishing as if drained from our blood, and the

Council continues to debate," he'd told Milos. "We are a doomed people, and they would rather deny it than to act."

It boggled his Holder's mind. Surely, the Eilaran Councilors had a responsibility to help and protect their people. The thought of his having left Tem Hold's people to their own devices suddenly reared up at him. Who was he to question the motives of the Eilaran Council when he had abandoned his own people, leaving them to fend for themselves and direct and defend their new form of governance in a land where Holders had always held power? Had he been so sure of their abilities to protect themselves? Or had his feelings for Kira colored his thinking so fully that he merely convinced himself he was doing the right thing in making such a drastic change and leaving the people of Tem Hold behind to deal with the consequences.

And now, when he was finally convinced that he needed to return home, here he was, trapped aboard an Outlander controlled vessel, sailing for who knew where and fighting to keep from giving up what little he knew of the Eilaran and *their new Matriar*ch.

Milos. Milos Tem. He heard Kira's voice in his mind. But the words she said made no sense to him. Murmured bits and pieces. Was this what it was like to hear others in one's head? Or was the closeness of the cell wearing on him? It must be the latter. In the muzziness of his half-waking state, Milos laughed quietly under his breath. Too bad he was not Eilaran. A shame he couldn't think-speak like so many of these people were able to despite their declining skills. It would be a useful tool at this moment.

Milos would simply have to make due with his usual skills.

He gripped the bars of his cage in frustration. This was worse than being trapped in the mists of Eilar. At least there, with the help of Kira's companions, he had been able to fight his way out. This was a physical prison, one that appeared impregnable. Yet, if he was going to help Kira and the people of Eilar, he needed to find a way out. He took in the dazed looks on his fellow prisoners. And he was going to need help.

Chapter 34

Kira stood in front of the Guardian's seat, the cold
stone at her back sending a chill throughout her body.
The Councilors arrayed themselves around the foot of the
dais as the Council First, supported by his Second, Zoshia,
climbed the polished stairs. The process seemed to take
forever, yet, all too soon for Kira the Chains of Office would
be settled upon her shoulders and she would take her place
as the Eilaran Matriarch in all ways. Fear shivered its way
across her skin and down her spine. She still had no idea
what the Chains of Office would do, how they might affect
her once the binding ritual was complete. Her mouth filled
with dust even as she reminded herself of the useless effort
of fearing the unknown. Had she allowed that sort of fear to
control her in the past, she would never have escaped from
Toril, never have had the time she'd had with Milos.

She barely heard the formal words the Council First
recited as he stood before her, his wizened face a blank
mask that hid his emotions, though Kira somehow sensed
that he was not altogether convinced of her willingness to
be ruled by the Council. There had been a lengthy debate,

she knew, about whether or not to entrust this power to her, but at Zoshia's urging the Council had finally come to an agreement; they would allow the Matriarch's heir to ascend to her place, but only as long as she acceded to their will and agreed to follow the formality of the oath taking.

She wondered once more about the Council Second's motives. Was it simply the desire to retain an unbroken line? To have another Matriarch sit upon the throne? Or was there something else that drove her, something more personal? Kira flicked a glance at Devira, who stood nearby, ready to take action as her attending Physica. Merely a precaution, she'd told Kira, but it did not allay the fear that shivered its way through her.

The Councilors stood arrayed at the foot of the stairs. Behind them, the rest of the room was filled to overflowing with people. Kira had no inkling of who most of them were, but none of them smiled. Every face seemed to wear a mask of seriousness that served to fill Kira with a trickling fear. As the First droned on, cold dread crept its clammy fingers across her skin. What had she been thinking when she committed herself to this?

She shuddered recalling what Devira had told her about the blood binding and the risk of breaking the oath she was preparing to take. How much free will would remain to her once the binding had taken place? Would she still be able to accomplish her own goals while keeping her word to be ruled by the Council? Well, she would know soon enough, she thought as the First held out his hand to her and Zoshia produced the crystal blade that would be used in the binding.

The First gestured for her to sit.

Kira took in a slow breath, then carefully settled herself into the Guardian's seat, expecting a wash of power that did not come. No visions, no velvet darkness to drown in. Merely a cold, hard seat that stole the warmth from her body despite the layers of cloth and cushions between her and the marble.

"Will you swear to be bound by the Guardian's oath?" the First intoned while taking her wrist and offering her outstretched hand to Zoshia.

"I swear it," she responded, her voice seemed to echo back at her from the walls of the Guardian's chamber. The chamber itself had been cleansed and repaired so that no signs remained of the struggle that had taken place within it. The marble had been polished and the shattered colored windows replaced. Even the steps of the dais shone with a light that seemed to emanate from within the stone. Probably another stone adept process, she thought, her agitated mind beginning to wander.

"Will you assume the mantle of Matriarch and receive the Chains of Office, to be guided and ruled by the Eilaran Council's wisdom in all matters?"

Kira stiffened at the words and steeled herself before replying. "I swear...to be guided by the Eilaran Council in all matters pertaining to the safety and guardianship of Eilar and its people." She bit her tongue to keep from smiling in satisfaction at the surprise that slipped across the First's face at her audacity of reciting the original oath, which Devira had given her, rather than the Council's newly wrought version. For a moment she thought, somewhat hopefully, that perhaps he would stop the ceremony, but before he regained his composure, Zoshia sliced the blade across Kira's palm, causing her to hiss in pain. The Second Council's face was a mask of determination. The cut was deeper than Kira had anticipated and the stinging wound made by the crystal knife made her wince, but she did not draw back her hand. All the while, she searched Zoshia's eyes, trying to discern her intentions, but the woman was inscrutable. "With this blood will you swear to be bound to the Guardian's seat and assume the rule of Eilar?" she intoned.

Zoshia held Kira's hand steady, allowing her palm to fill

with blood, as she gazed into her eyes.

"I do so swear it," Kira said, fighting against the sudden urge to flee. Her voice sounded thin in her own ears, yet somehow rang throughout the chamber for all to hear.

She braced herself as Zoshia slapped her palm down hard onto the arm of the Guardian's Seat, but the anticipated pain was nothing compared to the searing heat that traveled up her arm and across her chest. She heard rather than felt the back of her head crack against the back of the stone chair before her vision fogged and an aura of heat enveloped her. The world spun and power reached for her, gripping her and anchoring her, tying her to the land, making her one with the island. She was no longer separate, no longer an individual. She was connected to everything, much the way she had once been connected only to Kelmir and Vaith. Much the way she had been deeply and fully connected when the Matriarch had endowed her with her powers. Yet, this time, she had no guide and no control. And this binding was beyond her previous connection, less a connection and more like an extension—her into the land and the land into her.

She fought to remain conscious, to remain aware of herself, of the hard chair, the searing pain, but the draw of leaving her body grew stronger and she began slipping away, slipping into the grid of power lines that tore at her, pulling her in so many directions it seemed her mind would break. Her shield walls had already dissolved and the clamor of the world changed from a gentle thrumming to a pounding and crashing as of storm waves against rock. But she was no longer the rock, she was slipping away, eroding into sand, becoming nothing but tiny bits and pieces of who she once had been.

Before she could resolve the clamor of sensations, a burning cold settled upon her shoulders. The Chains of Office, she realized. They had proceeded with the ceremony, ignoring her semi-conscious state. The sharp cold helped to clear her mind and she hoped and prayed that these terrible sensations would cease. If not, she was sure her fate would be exactly the same as had been Matriarch Kyrina's.

She would go mad with the weight and oppression of her position.

Chapter 35

"Sanden," Milos whispered to the Eilaran sailor in the nearest cell.

She blinked at him, her brow wrinkling in confused thought. She raised her hand and scratched at her head. Her hair lay plastered against her skull with oil and sweat.

Milos realized with a start that he probably looked as bad or worse. And they were all beginning to smell from their time in the ship's hold without access to bathing, or basic necessities.

Her eyes drifted away from him, her lids drooping back down.

"Sanden," he tried again, but kept his voice low to avoid being overheard. They were all housed in the small cages, Milos and Dahl separate from the Eilaran. Though in their current state of stupor, it seemed hardly to matter.

Sanden opened her eyes wide and peered at him. "You're the Aestron warrior," she said, her face breaking into a smile. "You fought a dragon." A small laugh slipped out. "No. That's not right."

"Ssshhhh," Milos said, trying to keep her from attracting

the guard's attention. "You're Sanden, right?"

"Yeeees?" She sounded uncertain. "Yes. Sanden. That's... right." She squinted at him. "You're that Aestron warrior. The one that fought alongside the tiny, little dragon."

"Yes," Milos said, trying to keep the frustration from his voice. Getting through to her was going to be more difficult than he'd thought. He needed her clearer to help with his plan. "I'm thirsty," he said. "Do you have any water left?"

She stared around the small cell, searching until her fuzzy brain seemed to recognize the small water tin beside her.

"Here," she picked it up and tried to offer it to him, but knocked it against the bars, sloshing liquid out. "Oh." She pulled the tin back and stared into it for a moment, then raised it to her face, as if she intended to drink it.

"No, wait." Milos said, trying not to raise his voice above a whisper. "*I'm* thirsty, remember? You were going to give it to me."

She gazed up at Milos, then peered into the cup for another moment, her face going slack. Then, carefully, she set the tin on the deck and slowly pushed it through the bars of her cell, passing it to Milos.

"Thank you." He picked up the container and sniffed at it. There was a slight sweet odor. It reminded him of one of the herbs Kira had used to quiet some of her more difficult patients. So, the Eilaran water, as he thought, was drugged. He put his back to her, faced the ship's hull, and slowly emptied the vessel into a space between the damp planks where no one would notice the extra moisture.

He picked up his own water tin and, with a single guilty look at Dahl, emptied most of the contents into the Eilaran's container before passing it back to her. "Here," he said. "Drink up. I know you're thirsty."

Sanden took the tin and raised it high, pouring the contents into her mouth, spilling much of it down the front of her shirt in the process.

Milos sighed. This was going to take time. Time he hoped they had.

Chapter 36

Kira cupped her chin in her hands. She glared at the broken bits of Kavyn's stone that lay before her on the table. The room still smelled of singed fabric from the cloth they had been lying on during her last attempt to access them. She'd had to douse the cloth with the bowl of water she'd been using to try and transfer the information from one of the shards.

Kelmir peered at her from the opposite side of the room, his nose wrinkled in disgust at the smell. Vaith squawked from his perch at the window.

"Fine," Kira grumbled, standing and stretching her sore back as she crossed the room to open the shutters. Bright light poured into the room, startling her. "Oh," she groaned. "Is it already late morning?"

Vaith regarded her with disdain, as if to say she was behaving foolishly, before he leaped through the window and soared out over the keep's grounds. Feeling guilt, Kira hoped there were still a few mice or lazy voles out where they might make easy prey for the little wyvern.

"And you?" She shifted her attention to Kelmir. "I

suppose you merely wish to sleep after being out so late last night?"

Kelmir sprang gracefully onto the bed and curled his tail around his nose, blinked once, his eyes closing ever so slowly, then settled down to sleep.

The bed whispered to her of comfort, but Kira sighed and tuned back to the stone shards. She still had to figure out how to make this work. But the threads were too entangled, they were put together differently from the memories of her family's keep. Those were all more linear in thought and sounds, easy to trace and decipher. But this stone, it contained hundreds of thousands of tangled bits and pieces of information. They were all mixed together, like a tisane, or a healing formula that harnessed the combination of all the parts to make a more effective healing draught.

No. A formula. One that encompassed a multitude of components that when combined worked together to create a greater whole, a more efficient focusing tool. A keystone. But without knowing all of the ingredients, it would take a lifetime, perhaps many lifetimes, to unravel its secrets, and even if she had the time she might never be able to put them together again and align them the way they had been. And in the meanwhile, it would be like playing with fire.

She glared at the singed cloth in frustration and slammed her hand onto the table, wincing as she did at the sudden reminder that the ritualistic cut Zoshia had made with the crystal knife remained unhealed. She cradled her throbbing hand against herself, attempting to find a less painful position for it. Devira had told her it must heal on its own, that the Physics were not allowed to aid in the repair. Though when Kira had asked her why, Devira had merely shrugged. "Tradition is an odd thing. Like old habits. We often cling to them, despite not knowing whether they have a true purpose or no longer serve us."

Kira had the impression Devira was speaking of something else entirely, but she hadn't been able to figure out what it might be. Now, she gazed at the thin red line that streaked across the palm of her hand like a blazing trail while considering the time it would take, not to mention the blood, to decipher, untangle and transfer the contents of the keystone.

Of course, it couldn't be easy.

Once more, she had been a fool to believe she could walk into this land and become the leader they needed. She wasn't even politically capable enough to have kept the Council at bay, kowtowing to their wishes as soon as they threatened her. She had few allies and no understanding of how to rule. She should have found a way to keep Milos by her side. Trouble was, she had realized too late that she could have done exactly that. Traditions, like old habits, could be changed, couldn't they? She could have insisted on making him her equal. Could have ruled with him beside her. She was, after all, as far as anyone else knew, the true Matriarch of Eilar. Had, in fact, sealed that title with a bond of blood.

Done is done. Her need now was to focus on finding a way to fix the keystone and use it to restore the protections of Eilar.

She gazed at the shards for a long time, her eyes burning and bleary. She knew she should sleep, if not for her own health than for that of the child, but something kept pushing at her mind.

Exhaustion forced her to put her head down onto the table, resting one cheek against the cool wood, her eyes still locked on the puzzle that lay before her. In her exhausted mind, the bits of stone glimmered and called to her.

* * *

"Kira."

She started awake at the sound of his voice. "Milos?" She must have been dreaming. She wiped the sleep from her eyes and gazed around, but the room was far too dark. Could she have slept for so long? She rose to go to the window, expecting at least the glimmer of starlight, but in the darkness she stumbled into something soft and warm on the floor. She clutched at her heart when she heard the groan.

"Dreaming again. So glad you're here."

She sank to her knees beside him. "Milos! Oh, Milos. I'm not a dream, you are. But I don't care." She laid her head upon his warm chest and listened to the rhythm of his heart. "You're soaked," she said. "You'll catch your death."

He let out a small chuckle and slowly wrapped his arms around her. "That is pretty much the idea, I think."

She pulled away to peer at him. "What do you mean?"

"Never mind," he whispered, pulling her back down to him. "You're here. I've found you again. As long as I can keep you from him. That's all that matters."

Kira's body went icy. "Him?"

"The big ugly one. They say he's an exile. Wants revenge. I won't help him, Kira. I'll never help him. Despite our parting, nothing could ever make me betray you." He coughed and his breathing grew raspy as he fell away from her.

Kira tried to hang onto him, but light filled the room, and Milos faded from her arms. She found herself kneeling on the floor, sun still filtering in through the window, and a quizzical Kelmir eyeing her through one slit eye.

Had it truly been a waking dream? But no, it had been too real, too wrong. Wouldn't a dream be more perfect?

No. Somehow, despite the broken lines, she and Milos had found one another, had connected. She was certain of it.

She wrapped her arms about herself. If she could communicate with him, tell him the truth, that she still loved him, that she regretted the choices that had parted them, would it change anything? Perhaps not, but nonetheless, she needed him to know.

Chapter 37

Milos gritted his teeth against the pain. His head felt as if it would crack open and spill him out into the world, mind and soul. Sweat stuck his hair to his scalp and dripped into his eyes. The burning so severe, he could no longer tell whether they were open or closed.

He found himself in a strange place filled with a gray mist; a fog so dense he could no longer see his hand before his face. For a moment, panic rose in him. Then, he realized where he was, recognized the unfamiliar, turning it familiar.

His heart settled into its normal rhythm and his breathing slowed. He would not allow himself to fear this plane within his own mind. Would not be manipulated into wandering as if lost. He would not be fooled again.

He forced his mind elsewhere, recalling the forest near Tem Hold and the green clearing where Kira had first shown him the hunting talents of her companions, Vaith and Kelmir. He gazed in amazement as together they brought down a fat pheasant.

From far off he heard a voice calling him. The voice was familiar, but belonged to no one important. He settled in to watch the hunters in action once more. The shine of red hair against the greenery brought a smile to his lips, until searing agony sent him into total darkness once more.

The cold water brought him around, again.

"Wake up," a man's voice growled, right before a heavy hand slapped him across the face.

Milos refused to open his eyes. The meaty hand slapped him again, and again.

"He's awake," a voice said, followed by the sound of someone being shoved aside. "And I need him to stay that way."

Milos tilted his head sideways and cracked open an eye. Ekzarn, Milos recalled, the Eilaran outcast, exiled for some terrible crime committed before Kira had even been born. The man stood hunched over him, leaning his bent frame on an ornate cane. Was he more broken than he had been before? Or was it simply the swelling in Milos' eyes distorting the man's visage?

"So, you know a few tricks?" Ekzarn curled his lip in disgust. "Interesting. You're not of the blood. How did she teach you?"

Milos tried not to act surprised by the question. The less real information he offered up, the better. "Tricks?"

"Shielding takes practice." Ekzarn waved at one of his men. "You're not Eilaran. You shouldn't be so abled, and yet you are." He leaned closer.

A sailor dragged a wooden seat across the deck and set it in front of the beam where Milos was tied. The hunched man lowered himself onto the stool, leaning heavily upon his cane as he did. His body shook with palsy.

"How is it done?" Real curiosity colored Ekzarn's words.

Shielding? Milos thought. Is that what he had done? Did that mean he could keep the Eilaran out? Could he keep Kira a secret? But, no. The Aestron sailors had already told the man all they knew of Kira. And though Milos and Kira had kept much from them during their sea voyage, the crew's time in Eilar had been spent exposed to all manner of talk.

It was no secret amongst the Eilaran who Kira was, nor what she had become. But there was more personal information that only Milos was privy to, and *that* he would never willingly share. Especially, not with someone who clearly meant her harm. Despite the way she had treated him, Milos would never betray her, would never taint the memory of what they had had together. He would keep that to himself. He would keep it *for* himself.

He forced his eyes to focus on the man's face. In this case, an honest answer would do no harm. "I don't know what you mean."

"You may think your shielding a clever tactic," Ekzarn said, settling into the chair and taking the flagon of drink a sailor offered. "But it will only fail in the end. On the other side of things, you will be an interesting puzzle to disassemble. Though, you should know that, once taken apart, a mind does not quite fit back together again. Not as it once did, at any rate. A sorry thing, a mind poorly reassembled." The big man grinned. "Shall we begin?"

Milos closed his eyes against the sun and slipped away, seeking the bright meadow and green eyes in a pale face beneath short cropped red hair.

Chapter 38

"What is happening to me?" Kira rubbed her fingertips across her forehead.

"Dreams are a way of dealing with the things we don't always know how to deal with when we're awake." Devira tented her hands within her sleeves. "But, as this dream has so unnerved you, you might consider visiting a mentalist?"

"It wasn't a dream. I was awake. Only..." It had seemed so real.

"Are you certain? You've been pushing yourself hard. And what with your condition and the pressures of the Council, not to mention the ritual." Devira shrugged.

Kira placed her hands on her rounding belly. "Are you absolutely certain the ritual could not affect the child?" They had put every precaution in place, but still Kira felt unnerved.

"There have been numerous records of Matriarchs who were already with child when their rituals took place. None of the births had any issues that could be tied to the binding. Though..."

Kira sat forward. "What?"

"It's nothing." Devira tucked her hands tighter within her sleeves. "Your mother, Matriarch Kyrina, was said to have been conceived just before her mother's binding. There have been some that surmised that may have played a role in her ultimate...mental state. But they're merely rumors and speculation. Her mind didn't slip until..." Devira glanced up at her, lips pursed as if having caught herself before saying something she would regret.

"Until the assassination of my father? And my disappearance?" She rolled her shoulders. "Of course, how could there be any other place to rest any blame. It isn't like the weight of Eilar was upon her shoulders." She heard the bitterness in her own voice, but she didn't care. Let them think what they may. None of them could possibly know what it was like. The way the binding seared one's mind and body, the flaying of one's heart to be connected to everything and everyone while feeling so apart. She rested her face in her hands.

Devira rose and stood over her, placing a hand on her shoulder. The mere touch of the Physica helped to release some of the exhausted tension she'd been holding onto. "I know this is all overwhelming for you. You were not trained in our ways, were not prepared for all you have had to endure. But know that you are not alone, Kira. Never alone."

Tears would have been a relief, but Kira could not bring herself to allow them. She pushed herself up from the chair. "I need to rest. And then, I need to speak with Aertine, once more. There is more to this mystery than we know and we need to begin to put the pieces together, sooner rather than later." She shuffled over and eased her way onto the bed beside Kelmir, who shifted enough to allow her access to the warmth where he had been sleeping, then she fell instantly into a deep slumber.

Chapter 39

Milos reached for her hand, their fingers touching, braiding together and locking the way they used to. The softness of her palm against his caused a shiver to roll up his arm and across his heart. How he'd missed this simple intimacy, her hand in his. He treasured the feel of her cool, slender fingers against his.

"I've missed you," she murmured, her words tinged with regret.

"And I, you," he said, keeping his eyes on their hands, afraid to look away lest she fade from him once more.

"This feels so much like a dream." Her voice held a hint of wonderment.

"Don't. I want to believe you're here." He needed to believe this was real. At least, for this moment.

A startled surprise filled her face. "I am. At least, it seems that way." She leaned against him, placing her head upon his shoulder.

He wrapped his arms around her and stroked her back, inhaling the scent of her.

She pulled away and gazed into his face. "I don't

understand it, but..."

He shook his head. "Do you remember," he asked, stroking his fingers along her cheek, "when we stood upon the deck of the Sunfleet. Your eyes shimmered like the stars upon the sea."

"Mmmmm." She relaxed against him as his fingers trailed down her neck. "I don't think you're recalling the starlight." Her voice was husky.

"No," he admitted, letting his hand drift down to her shoulder.

She stiffened under his touch. "You're in danger." Her eyes filled with panic. "Milos. It's not a dream."

"Hush," he told her. "We're together again. That's all that matters."

"No. You must protect yourself—"

He put a finger to her lips. "We have each other."

Kira's face fell. "It may not be enough. He's coming for us."

Milos started. "Who?"

"He's been searching for me, and we are a beacon, now." She sat up and pulled his hand to her stomach. "We shine in the darkness and draw his hate. And he'll use whatever means he can to destroy us. All of us."

Milos stared at his hand, then finally tore his gaze away, clapping his eyes onto hers. "I don't understand."

Her face shimmered, growing hazy and indistinct.

"I need you to know..." Kira's voice faded into the distance.

Milos spluttered and gasped, lungs searing as they hauled him up out of the water. His eyes burned as he blinked away the salty water. The ropes that bound him cut into the flesh beneath his arms and his wrists chafed from the wet bindings. He'd tried worrying at them with his teeth until the air had gone from his lungs and he had barely enough strength to reach up and grab the rope to pull his face above water as they'd dragged him alongside the ship.

174

His arms ached with the effort, but this time he had at least remained conscious. Or had he? The vision of Kira came back to him. Each of her visits seemed more real than the last.

He tried to shake the thoughts from his head, but the water dragged at him, the ship's wake cresting over him, filling his ears and nose and mouth.

No, there was something too real about her visitations. It was as if they had somehow become connected, the way she and her animal companions were connected. Had the pillar done that when he'd touched it? Certainly *something* had changed him. Something that served to agitate Ekzarn. Especially the part that had made him unreadable to the exiled Eilaran.

She knew, though. About Ekzarn. But what was it she meant about them being a beacon?

His arms cramped and he sucked in a breath as his head slipped once more below the salty froth.

Chapter 40

"So, you toyed with our family's heritage merely to discover it did you no good. What an odd turn." Aertine folded her arms across her chest.

"There's no need to be sarcastic," Devira said.

Truth be told, Kira thought, the Physica never scolded, but she could certainly make one feel they had been. She waved the thought aside. "She's right. Though, it wasn't my intent to 'toy' with anything. I was merely researching the problem in the hope to repair two stones with one solution."

"Nicely put." Aertine smirked. "But maybe now you'll listen when I tell you something can't be done."

"I agree the approach is wrong, but I still believe something can be done."

Aertine shook her head. "I've already told you, it's beyond my skills to discern how this stone was created."

"I know that, but have you considered repairing it?"

Aertine snorted. "Repairing it? Have you looked at it? It isn't a cracked bowl that can merely be mended."

"Hear me out," Kira said. She glanced at the door and lowered her voice. "What if we treated it like a puzzle box.

Put the pieces..."

"Shards and slivers, you mean." Aertine frowned.

"All right, but we found them all, didn't we? Once Devira had been removed for healing, I had the room closed off. We searched the room before anyone else touched a thing. If we can manage to put them back together—"

"If? Don't you mean how? There is no glue to hold together a stone like that. The pieces are far too small, they would need..."

"They would need what, Sister?" Devira was suddenly alert.

"A moment," Aertine murmured, "give me but a moment." She strode over to the table and leaned forward, staring at the broken bits of stone. "It might be done. Possible. But workable?" She shook her head and nudged the fragments with a finger tip. "And if there is any bit missing?" She stood up and looked Kira in the eye. "The risk is too great."

"For whom?" Kira asked. "If it be the wielder, then I will take that risk. Each day we wait to find a solution brings us closer to losing this land and its people."

"But this keystone, as you call it, could destroy you. And what little remains of our defenses. No. I'll not be a part of it."

"Defenses? Have you been sleeping? We have no defenses. Kavyn saw to that." Kira held up her hand. "Don't ask me how I know. I simply do. Something, someone, is coming. For me. For all of us. And without this keystone, we are defenseless." She tried to push past the memory of what had happened in the Guardians room, but the images roiled up and pummeled her mind until Devira placed a healing hand upon her back.

"Breathe," the Physica told her. "Breathe and let go."

Kira did as she was told. "Thank you," she said, shaking herself loose from the unbidden memories. "I'm fine. But, Aertine, you need to understand that whoever helped to create this keystone, Kavyn was not working alone. And whoever aided him is still out there. And he still wants..." the word came bubbling up from her waking dream with Milos "... revenge."

Aertine gave her a hard look. "Who?"

"I don't know, precisely." Kira paced the floor, stopping at the place where she had found Milos in the waking dream. "I only know he is some kind of exile."

Devira's face fell and all color drained from her as she sank into the nearest chair. "It's not possible."

"What?" Aertine asked. "What's not possible?"

Devira shook her head. "I am not at liberty to discuss this. It is Council business that I should not even be privy to, except that..."

"Except that what?" Aertine prodded.

"Except that it involved someone in my care." Devira focused her gaze on the floor.

"But you are privy to this information," Kira said. "And if it affects this land, this people, I need to know."

Devira wrapped her arms about herself. "There was once one among us...someone with great power." She turned away, her body shaking.

"What is it, Sister?" Aertine asked. She placed a hand upon Devira's arm and coaxed her around to face them.

"He would have become a tyrant," she told Kira. "The uses to which he would have put that power..." Devira's face filled with a dark anger the likes of which Kira had never seen before. "Your mother...Matriarch Kyrina, fed his ego. She wooed him into sharing his secrets. Once she had the evidence she needed, enough to prove the threat he posed, she informed on him to the Council. He was exiled." The normally calm and centered Physica shook with emotion. "His skills. The power he can command. If he has had a hand in any of this, then we must find a way to protect this land and its people, and we must do so quickly."

178

Chapter 41

Aertine stood among the wreckage of her family's ruined memory keep and held the small crystal in her hand. Devira had snatched it up from the table as they'd left and thrust it at her once they were outside the keep.

"Here," she'd said, offering the crystal with her broken fingers.

Aertine had stepped back, pain twisting in her gut. "No. Devira. You know how I feel about it."

"Yes, I do. You have made certain of that," Devira accused.

"What is that supposed to mean?" Aertine hissed.

"I'm sorry." Devira held the stone up and gazed at it. "That was ugly of me, but it pains me to see you wallow."

"I? Wallow?"

"All these years. You suffer over the loss of our family's keep as if it is the only thing to be mourned in all the realm." Devira closed her gnarled fingers around the stone. "And I understand your pain. Share it, though you would not have it so."

"I see. So, the many years that you spent seeking favor

of the Matriarch, tending her cares, mending her hurts, patronizing the one person in all the world that deserved your hate, that is how you shared in my loss?"

"Aertine. Sister. Who are you?"

"What are you talking about?"

"Do you recall who you are?"

Aertine straightened her back and squared her shoulders. "I am Mistra Aertine, stone and metal adept."

"Not what you do, but who you are."

"I...I don't know what you're asking."

"Yes, you do."

Aertine hadn't known what to say. She'd stood staring at her sister in confusion.

"Take it," Devira had insisted, forcing the stone into Aertine's hand. "And remember who you are."

Aertine had glowered at the stone, ready to throw it into the river, but Devira placed her hands around Aertine's and cupped the stone between them. "You are not alone, Aertine," she said. "You have never been alone." Then she had turned and walked away.

Now, Aertine stood in the dying light, tears spilling from her eyes. The memories Kira had pulled from the shattered memory keep whispered from the stone in her hand. Over and over again, she heard her mother's laughter at the joke her father had just made.

Though she had sifted among the ruins for years, trying to piece back together the puzzle of the familiar grown distant, she had not found what she had been searching for. Before this, Aertine had forgotten that moment, had lost it along with so many other memories that had faded with the passage of time. But now, that tiny memory stirred the recollection of that day. The last one she and her sisters had spent with their parents as a family before their duties had split them off.

She felt her heart melt and in that instant an unexpected change came over her. "This," she murmured. The piece of her that had been missing since the disappearance of their sister and the destruction of their family's Memory Keep seemed to slide back into place inside her. It repaired the cracks on her heart, the brokenness that had chafed like a jagged bit of quarry stone, the roughness that had invaded her and had not let go.

Until now.

Chapter 42

Milos surfaced from the dream once more, raising a swollen eyelid enough to glimpse his surroundings. He was in the Captain's cabin. Propped up on a stool, bound hand and foot.

Across the room, Ekzarn leaned back in an ornate chair. His eyes glittered eerily in the lamplight.

Milos glanced to the window, wondering what time it was, then realized how little it really mattered now that he'd lost track of the days. A derisive snort escaped him.

"Something amuses you?" Ekzarn leaned forward. His face appeared more gaunt than before, hunger emanated from him, but not a belly hunger. It wasn't food Ekzarn craved.

Milos let his head fall forward, his mind reaching once more for the place inside where his memories of Kira seemed so real.

"Yes," Ekzarn murmured. "Do go back to your reverie."

The need in his voice penetrated Milos' muzzy brain and pulled him back. He forced both eyes open and peered at the Eilaran, looking closer. The need that poured off the man was almost physical. It pushed at Milos, pressing against him, chilling the sweat that beaded on his brow. After all the trouble he'd gone to before to pull Milos back from the safety of his thoughts, why would Ekzarn suddenly push him to let go.

Milos wasn't sure, but he knew that whatever it was the Eilaran wanted, it couldn't be good. Not for anyone, except Ekzarn. But why this? What might he gain from Milos drifting back to his memories? Was it merely information about Kira? Did he think he might be able to break through the barrier he claimed Milos had created inside his mind and gain more knowledge?

Or was it something else?

The remembrance of his dreaming visits with Kira, the realness of them, sent a rush of anxiety coursing through him. His limbs twisted, straining against the ropes that held him as her words the last time he'd dreamed of her thrust a spear of worry through him. *We shine in the darkness and draw his hate. We are a beacon.*

She had told him she was not a dream. That her visits were real. What if it was true? What if they truly were connecting? Might the exiled Eilaran be able to use that connection? Anything seemed possible with these people. Milos couldn't let that happen. He would not allow himself to be used against Kira. He had to find a way to warn her away. The next time he saw her...

Suddenly, the entire notion seemed like the musings of a lunatic. Was he finally losing his mind to the tortures inflicted upon him? He might have laughed if not for the anticipation on Ekzarn's face. But no. The Eilaran knew something, had a reason to want Milos to drift back into that space, the place where he might reconnect with Kira's memory. And no matter what, Milos would do everything in his power to deny him what he wanted.

Chapter 43

Aertine wiped the sweat from her brow. The heat of the workshop had become stifling, but she dared not stop in the midst of her task, dared not falter. Based on the Matriarch's warnings, the fate of everything Aertine held dear was at stake. She would not let exhaustion or doubt keep her from completing this work.

She focused on the shards of the keystone. With her work on the shattered memory keep, Matriarch Kira had not only unlocked the secret of transferring the stored memories, but had opened the gates and paved a way for delving deeper into the making of the stone. Aertine was at once amazed and abashed at Kira's discovery of a pathway into the complex art behind this working of the land's power. Though they still had much to learn, the foundation was now laid for repairing and perhaps even recreating the land's defenses. If only Aertine could finally manage to piece back together this tool.

The door opened and she forced herself not to look away from the work.

"Mistra?" Varnon crept near. "I wish to help."

"Varnon. You need to leave." Aertine bit her lower lip and shook her head. "I must concentrate." Sweat ran down her face, dripping from her brow and into her eyes. She blinked back the sting of it.

A gentle hand touched a damp cloth to her forehead, her cheek, the cool of it not quite startling, but enough to bring the stone back into focus.

"You need my help."

True. His skill would be invaluable, but she couldn't allow it. He had a lifemate to consider now. "You've a growing family that needs you." The risk of going against the Council...

"My loyalty also lies here," he said, as if reading her thoughts. "With the safety of our people, and our loved ones. Let me help with that."

Aertine nodded in understanding. She should have realized he would know, would have put all the clues together and worked out that what she was working on had to do with the land's defenses. "Then make yourself useful," she told him, repeating the phrase she had often used when he had first come to her as a mere lad just beginning to understand the working of his own skills and the need to exercise them. "Stoke the fire."

He stepped away, drew on his leather apron and gloves, then reached for the fire iron to stir the coals. He moved the foot bellows over to his side of the box and gently peddled it, sending in fresh air to feed the fire and coax the red heat of making back into the coals. "What will the heat do to the gem? Stone does not temper as metal does."

"I am using the fire and pressure to imbue the stone with a higher density," Aertine responded. "It is something I have toyed with before. Only then, I was merely attempting to develop more efficient stones of holding." She wiped at her brow once more. "This is altogether different than anything I have ever done."

"Then I will learn much by helping." He smiled as he

fanned the flames.

Aertine felt the tug of a smile pulling at the corners of her own mouth. "Indeed. But only if you pay heed to what we are about and do not let your mind wander."

Chapter 44

"Our informants have confirmed it," Councillor Teldin said. "The Matriarch continues to research the secrets of Kavyn's device."

Several of the Councilors gasped audibly and Zoshia stiffened. Ancestors blood! This Matriarch was proving to be as stuboorn as her predecessor.

"This must stop. The Council has forbidden it," one of them shouted.

"I knew the binding ritual was a mistake."

"She needs to be reined in."

"Yet, what recourse do we have to end her persistence?" another asked. "We should have acted before the formal binding took place."

The assembled councilors all began talking at once. Heated discussions grew loud. All agreed that the Matriarch had no right to behave in such a manner. But none agreed on what must be done.

Finally, Zoshia could take it no more. Complaints would not provide a solution to their current predicament. "Yes, she is guilty of dissemblance." She thought of Devira and her devotion to her charge and attempted to soften the accusations. "Remember, she is young and was not raised within our culture. She does not fully fathom our ways."

"Her ignorance does not excuse her willful defiance of the Council. Especially after taking the binding oath," Councilor Vestyne declared.

"Councillor Zoshia," the First intoned. His growing anger permeated his aura and suffused his voice. "We have not forgotten that it was your actions that allowed the binding to take place...despite the tempered oath."

Zoshia felt her face heat. She'd known it was a risk to provide the original wording, but Devira had been so persuasive and, after all they had been through, Zoshia could not bring herself to deny her lifemate on this. "But the response she gave was recited from the formal script."

She had done her best not to sound as if she were schooling the First, but he erupted with ire. "It appears that your vision is clouded in regards to this...this renegade Matriarch."

A hush fell over the Council and Zoshia stared at the First. Surprise at his change in demeanor sent all thoughts of debate out of her head. His words had held more anger than she had ever heard him express in all their years on the Council, even in the private moments behind closed doors where they had discussed issues not as First and Second, but nearly as peers.

"We have not yet tested her strength, her initial refusal of the Guardian's Seat and the Chains of Office kept us from that assessment, but even when she was untrained her skills were formidable. Do not forget what happened at the inquiry," Vestyne said.

"And now that she has been blood-bound? Even with the Chains of Office as an anchor, her connection will only be that much stronger, her power..." Councilor Daryk let the rest of the thought hang in the air before them.

Zoshia closed her eyes and forced herself under control.

Despite all her efforts to balance her loyalties, everything she held dear was now poised on the edge of destruction. Is this what it had come to? Was this the Council that she had spent everything to support? Was this truly worth the cost that she had paid?

As they continued to argue and discuss what might be done, she saw Devira and the hurt in her eyes, the angry way they had parted and the continuing coldness between them since that time.

She shook away the memory, opened her eyes and gazed around the room at each of her fellow Councilors, their serious faces, the fear that showed in their eyes. She thought of the pride she had experienced upon being raised to the Eilaran Council, all her years of service, and the faith that had been placed in her.

She held out her hand to speak, waiting until the First recognized her. "How then shall we proceed?" she asked, her steady voice resonating throughout the formal Council chamber.

Meryk rapped on the floor with his staff. "We must find a way to undo what has been done. And we will bring the might of the Council to bear, if need be."

Chapter 45

"Milos, I'm so sorry." She stroked his cheek and kissed his brow, the touch of her soft lips spreading warmth throughout his body. He wanted so much to believe that she was real and not a mind trick that Ekzarn was playing on him. But, dream or no, he could not risk Ekzarn discovering how much he still loved her. And if these visitations were real. If she had somehow managed to find a way to reach him so far across time and space, then it was that much more dangerous for her.

"Kira," Milos said. "You cannot come to me again like this."

"But—"

What had Ekzarn said about his having learned some tricks? Had the pillar truly endowed him with something akin to the Eilaran's skills? Or was it something else? Either way, he must find a way to block her out. "Shhhhh." He placed the tip of his finger over her lips. "It is too dangerous for you." There was still time. He would find a way to turn the exile aside from Eilar. Or die in the effort. Anything to keep from being the cause of harm to her.

"He is coming for you," he murmured, pushing her away and closing off all thoughts of her. "You must forget me."

He woke to see Ekzarn seated before him once more.

"I'll wear you down in time," the Eilaran outcast snarled. "Keep him from sleeping until I return." Ekzarn pulled himself up with his walking stick and dragged himself away.

Milos watched until the Eilaran reached his quarters and went inside. Then he began to make quiet retching sounds.

"What are you about?" His guard yanked him up by the back of the collar.

"Sick." Milos made as if to heave his guts across the deck.

"Not on my watch," grumbled the marine, dragging Milos with him to the side of the ship. Milos wormed his fingers into his pocket and, while gagging and spitting, tossed the crystal over the side of the ship and watched it sink out of sight. It seemed a shame to do so. It might not be the root of his visions, but then again, as Marquon had said. It was a small piece of Eilar and who knew what magic it might contain?

* * *

"No!" Kira woke with a start, head pounding, damp hair clinging to her scalp. She had finally reached him, finally found a way to communicate with him, to convince him her visitations were not merely dreams, and he had shut her out. Why? He had seemed so happy to have her with him. What did he mean too dangerous? How did he know of the threat to her? How could he? She shoved the coverlet aside and slid from the bed.

Vaith flapped his wings and pushed his concern at her. Beside her, Kelmir stood, prepared to attack whatever or whoever might come near.

I'm fine, she told them, realizing even as she thought

it that it was a lie. She wasn't fine, would never be fine. Not until she had managed to put things right. Both here in Eilar—she rubbed her rounding belly—and between her and Milos.

Chapter 46

Another sleepless night passed and Aertine found her mind spinning. Each failure had brought with it yet one more discovery of what would not work. Yet, they still had not arrived at a complete process that would. Though the smaller attempts had given them hope. Each time they sought to combine the workings into the pattern they had sussed from the broken stone, the entire mess would go awry.

She couldn't fathom what was lacking, other than the tiny sliver of stone they had been unable to locate, but something was, and it was up to her to determine what.

But she'd tried everything she knew. Everything except using the hazardous combination of extreme heat and pressure to rebuild what they could.

And now here she was risking everything in one last attempt. If she failed in this attempt, if the process she planned to employ destroyed the power within the stone... Better not to think on that and focus on the task at hand.

She gripped the heavy tongs and shoved the metal fitting into the water, dousing it. Steam rose, clouding her vision as the metal cooled. She pulled it out and set the still warm fitting upon the workbench, placing it into the slotted end of the mold. The shards rattled as they shifted within the framework. It still worried her that they had not found that missing tiny sliver. They had searched and re-searched the Guardian's keep, but with no luck. And something so thin and tiny, barely the size of a nail clipping, could have been carried out on the tip of a shoe or the hem of a robe with no one the wiser.

But Devira's anxiety had grown with each passing moment spent in attempting to locate the tiny shard. Kira had finally pushed for them to forge ahead without it, though her confidence in her ability to overcome that missing bit of such a powerful and unknown tool must surely have been feigned. Ignoring the growing apprehension in her own heart, Aertine had moved forward.

There had been too many trials to count with too many stones. Stones she had instructed Varnon to break and smash in countless ways. Few had shown the promise she had hoped for until, with great trepidation, she took the remade bit of memory Kira had given her and smashed it on the ground. It was a hard loss, especially after the hope that had been stirred in her heart by the memories it contained, but her sacrifice was small in comparison to what was at stake.

By wrapping the stone in a filigree mesh and placing it into a heavier fitting, she'd been able to reconnect some of the threads. Though, according to Kira, there were random delays in connecting with and accessing the bits of information, particularly in one of the threads, which caused each of her attempts to work with the stone to fail. That delay continued to worry her. Could it be caused by the lack of solid stone, the small gaps filled by the metal filaments in the repairs she'd made? And would this process finally repair the stone and make it usable, or destroy it completely? There was no way now to be certain, but she hoped, nay, prayed, for the former.

"Mistra," Varnon said in a low voice. "Shall I reset the shards?"

She grunted. "Be quick about it, the crucible is nearly at temperature. I don't want to lose the moment and have to start again. I've not much left in me."

At her elbow, he resettled the broken bits of the focus stone, fitting them back into the order she'd determined after too many trials to count. If they didn't get this right, there would be no more attempts. Once the original shards were locked within the metals, connected by the mesh, their previous experiments had shown that reheating them would destroy whatever might remain of their power resonance. Sweat trickled down her back as the metal grew near to bursting aflame.

"Varnon?"

"One moment more." He grabbed the metal pincer and used it to tuck the last bit into its proper place.

"Now, Varn." She lifted the crucible from the coals.

"Pour." He pulled his hand aside just as the glowing metal streamed into the mold, and joined his mind with hers, following her lead. This was the crucial part, the melding of the shards into place with the metal connectors while simultaneously providing the energy to rebind the whole into an intact artifact once more.

The last of the molten metal slid into the mold, covering the stone shards and she set the crucible aside.

"Ease on," she told him, her voice strained from the exertion. "Just a bit more pressure."

The stone hummed as the precious metal filled the cracks between the broken pieces, creating new connections. She was thankful for Varnon's years of apprenticeship, knowing the urge to use too much force was held at bay only through rigorous training and practice. Even maintaining the steady flow of energy would tax his every reserve, but as much as she always pushed him to be better, she trusted his control.

Depended on it.

As the metal cooled, the resonance grew in intensity until the power of it screamed deep into muscle and grated against bone. it seemed to rise and rise, the peak always just a hint away.

"Mistra?"

"Don't let up." Her words grated through gritted teeth.

Aertine tensed, fighting against the urge to draw away at the crucial moment. Varnon's brow drew down and the muscles in his jaw clenched. She'd been reluctant to allow him to help, but was sorely glad of his assistance now that the task neared completion.

Focus. She needed to focus. If what the Matriarch had said was true, then they needed to succeed. Now. This final effort was so far beyond anything Aertine had ever done. The risk was great. If she failed, if the stone was ruined, there would not be another attempt.

A low sound rose from Varnon's throat, matched by a thrumming from the stone, which glowed beneath their hands and vibrated so hard it felt as if it were attempting to escape them, as if it had a mind, a will, of its own.

"Concentrate," Aertine murmured from between her clenched teeth. Her jaw hurt with the strain. The muscles of her body seemed to contract until her body began to cramp and she feared a spasm that would force her to release her hold before the work was finished.

It seemed the seasons would turn before they would be done. The small room closed in on her, gray shadows pricked the edges of her vision and she realized she was holding her breath. She forced her lungs to contract and expand, and slowly the darkness receded, but still the energy siphoned from her into the stone.

Would there ever be an end to it? Would they be drained dry? She flicked her eyes up to Varnon His face was pale, eyes closed tight, the strain pulling his skin taut, but he held on. And if her apprentice could stand the strain, then so too could his master.

Finally, with a shudder, the stone calmed and her body unclenched. She raised her eyes up to see Varnon staring down at their work in wonder.

"Is it done?" he rasped.

Aertine nodded, her throat too dry to speak. It was good he had come. She would not have had the strength to do this work alone.

Slowly and carefully, they set the newly remade keystone onto its waiting stand to finish cooling and collapsed against the wall to catch their breath and gaze at what they had accomplished.

They sat slumped, stunned and bedraggled, but filled with the joy that comes from the hope of success.

Aertine's mouth felt as dry as the ashes in the cinder bucket. "Never have I felt so spent." Her words scraped against her tongue like snakeskin against sandstone.

Varnon's eyes were closed, his head tilted back against the wall. "Nor I."

She rolled her shoulders to ease the cramps that had settled in and around her neck and back, then let out a small huff of relief. "I'll have need of my sister's skills this night."

"But we have done the impossible." His voice was filled with wonder and the certainty of youth.

Aertine quirked up the side of her mouth. "Clearly, not impossible." She licked her dry lips, felt the elation drain away from her. "And we are not yet certain of our results. It remains to be seen if the stone will work as intended." She pushed herself up, easing herself to a standing position. "If it does not stand up to the use the Matriarch intends…"

His eyes popped open and he leaned toward her in earnestness. "Will it hold, do you think?"

She thought about the power she had sensed the Matriarch pull from a single line. Would the stone hold such power? Or would the Matriarch's lack of training be the undoing of their work?

Exhaustion cascaded over her entire being, but there was no more time to waste. The stone must be brought to the Matriarch before the Council realized what they were up to. "We shall soon find out."

Chapter 47

Ekzarn jolted upright, back arched, chin raised to the sky at the thrum of power that juddered through his bones, a twisted song of pain and ecstasy that struck without warning. It rose up, building upon itself until his eyes leaked with the intensity of it. *Remade. Remade. Remade.* Though the song contained a discordant note, he welcomed its unexpected tenor. His tool. His focal point. His way in. Resurrected from destruction.

He reached for the line of power, but it slid from his grasp, fading into the distance. He doubled over, the wrenching sense of loss a punch to his gut. Sweat poured from his forehead to drip into his fisted hands. Damn Kavyn's meddling stupidity. Damn his locked mind! Without a mind to connect him, and with the shattered lines keeping him at bay, he would need to find another way in, another way to access the power of Eilar.

He wiped a sleeve across his damp brow, then rose unsteadily and gazed out the window at the undulating, blue-green sea.

He closed and opened his fist, knuckles cracking, as the

memory of power shivered through his blood. Across the watery expanse lay his destiny, seemingly as impatient for him as he for it.

And nothing would keep them apart.

Chapter 48

Kira hefted the keystone in her hand, testing its weight and eyeing the repairs that Aertine had managed. The stone emanated a strange vibrating power that surged outward and enveloped her hand with a tingling sensation, like the buzzing of a thousand bees.

"It seems...different."

Aertine pursed her lips for a moment, then shrugged. "It is as whole as we have the means to make it. But I cannot guarantee—"

"That it won't shatter the moment I attempt to use it?" Kira shook her head. "I heard you the first time you said it, and the time after that. But do we have any other choice?"

Aertine shook her head. "I do not pretend to understand how you do what you are able, nor how you can know what is coming. But I will do my part to keep the stone intact as well as it is within my power to do so."

"Then you will proceed against the Council's wishes? They are not without their means of power," Devira warned her. "Zoshia was not bluffing when she came to warn us. The focused power of so many..."

Kira's stomach soured at the thought of her time before the interrogators, but the memory of Ekzarn's threats steeled her. "Should I sit by and watch as this land and its people are overtaken by a monster?"

"You may risk your life," Devira said, concern in her voice. "That is your choice. But what of your unborn child?"

Kira caressed her swollen belly, staring at her changing body in wonder. "He will not stop until he destroys both me and my child. Cowering will not save any of us. There is no option but to fight." She locked eyes with Devira. "And if what Zoshia has told you is true, the Council plans to come against me, no matter that the binding is complete. The only question that remains is where your loyalty now lies. Will you once more stand with the Matriarch? Or will you add your power to the Council?" Her voice was soft, but she knew what she was asking.

Aertine spluttered and her face reddened. "You question my sister's loyalty? After everything...?"

"Sister. Peace." Devira folded her broken hands within her robes and set her mouth in a firm line. "As with the Matriarch before, I will do all that I can to protect you, and your unborn child, even from yourself." She strode across the room and pulled back the bedclothes, then stepped aside. "Meanwhile, you must still rest and care for yourself and..." she waved a hand at Kira's midsection.

Kira forced herself not show her surprise at Devira's commanding tone.

"Please be so kind as to heed your Physica's advice." Aertine nodded meaningfully at the bed. "There is still much to do before we may even begin to field a defense. And we will need your strength."

Kira wished for an end to all of this, to be able to do whatever was needed now, rather than later. But her body ached, her limbs were heavy, and she longed for sleep. They were right, of course. As a Healer herself, she knew full well what a body was and was not capable of. "I defer to my Physica," she said as she crossed the room, sliding off her dressing gown before slipping into bed and allowing Devira to pull the covers up to her chin.

Kelmir leaped lightly onto the bed and curled at her feet as Vaith settled upon the bedpost above her head. Their closeness comforted her.

"I've tripled the number of shielding stones around the room, and our strongest adepts have charged them to capacity," Aertine said. "You should be well protected. Though, I would prefer it if you would take my advice and sleep in one of the isolation cells."

Kira shivered at the memory of the emptiness of the soundless room she'd spent her hours in awaiting her time before the inquirers. As much as she needed to keep herself shielded, the closeness of Vaith and Kelmir was too much a comfort now to forego. "No. I will not be terrorized into hiding in a hole. What you have managed will do." She let herself relax against her pillows. In truth, the energy that normally pressed against her had been noticeably dampened, and she already felt relief seeping into her, the stress of holding so much at bay slipping away.

She glanced over to where Vaith and Kelmir rested. "If anything should happen to me..."

"They will be well cared for," Aertine said. "I have already recruited my apprentice to the task, though he knows not exactly what he has promised."

Kira thought about it for a moment. "He was smitten with Vaith. I only hope his willingness carries to Kelmir, as well." She tried to focus her thoughts away from where they were headed. "I will convey my wishes to my companions."

Devira settled herself onto the narrow window seat. "It may not come to that," she insisted, though her words lacked conviction.

"Will you not heed your own advice?" Kira chided.

"When my patient is at rest, so will I be," Devira told her. "And when the time comes, I will do whatever is needed to keep you whole," Devira said.

"As stubborn as ever, Sister." Aertine shook her head, but there was a gentleness in her voice that Kira had not heard before.

Devira gazed out at the night sky. "We may change our minds, but not our natures."

Her words made Kira think of Heresta. She closed her eyes and saw once again the small cottage in the little meadow where she had lived and trained with her mentor.

She saw it, not as it had appeared the final time she had visited Heresta on the day the old woman had returned to the wheel, but as it had been when she was younger, with the garden in bloom, the stream babbling merrily past, smoke rising from the chimney, and the smell of savory stew emanating from inside.

Kira's whirring mind continued to churn. "And the others? Will any of them support us, do you think?" She tried to keep the worry from her voice.

Aertine held out her hands in a signal of acceptance of what might come. "We can only ask."

"But some of us are much more persuasive than others," Devira said with a nod at her sister.

The way the bond between her aunts had been restored caused Kira to think of Milos. She wished they could have made their peace with one another face to face rather than from such a distance, that he hadn't closed himself off from her as he had. She pushed away her wishful thinking and glanced once more across the room at her aunts, her allies.

They all knew what the stakes were. They had discussed it enough. Now, it was a matter of making the last of their preparations and waiting for the storm break.

Chapter 49

Milos waited in silence as the Eilaran skilled sat quietly and did what appeared to be nothing. But somehow Milos could sense the energy they drew into themselves. It vibrated in the air around them. If he were able to leave his cell and draw closer, would he be able to hear it? Might he even be able to hear their thoughts the way they seemed to do when they shared their minds with one another?

He wondered what it might be like to do so while awake. Would he be able to communicate with Kira no matter where she might be? He did not regret casting Marquon's stone from him and, hopefully, his last connection with Kira. That had been a necessary act. But still the loss pained him.

"Aestron." Someone hissed from across the way. "We are ready."

Finally, Milos thought. It had taken days for the all Eilaran to awaken from their drugged state. He wasn't certain he could hold out any longer against the punishment doled out by Ekzarn and his Outlanders. "Dahl." he shook the boy's shoulder.

The young man opened his eyes, blinking as he reoriented

himself. "I was dreaming we were back home. My mam was just about to ladle up a huge helping of her fish stew," he said groggily and with more than a little complaint in his tone.

"My apologies." Milos braced himself for his part. "I need you to call the guard and tell him I've taken ill."

Dahl sat up in a rush, eyes suddenly clear and a worried expression on his face. "You're sick?"

"Not yet, but I'm going to be." Once Milos explained what he wanted Dahl to do, he braced himself and raised the bowl of sour leftovers he'd been saving for the last few days, tilted his head back and forced himself to swallow.

Chapter 50

Zoshia stood in the doorway of the Council Chamber and forced herself to breathe. The summoning had been so sudden, she'd barely had time to make herself presentable. Her consternation at being called at such a late hour was quickly replaced by surprise at finding the entire Council assembled upon her arrival and the fear of having been found out. But the revelation that she had been watched, spied upon, had turned that emotion to anger.

"Zoshia Valpine, by breaking with the Council, you have broken your oath."

"No," Zoshia said. She faced them down from across the room, though she knew she would be no match should they decide to come against her. "My oath was not made to this Council. My oath was to the people and the land of Eilar. And that oath, I have never broken."

The First shook his head. "I am sorely disappointed in you, Zoshia. Of all the Councilors, I believed you to be among the most loyal. But this breach of conduct cannot be allowed to pass."

"Strip her of her position!" shouted Daryk.

"Charge her with treason," Vestyne spat.

"Treason?" Zoshia kept herself in check, even as a part of her longed to laugh at them. "I stand for the Matriarch," she said. "How then is that treason?"

Councilor Vestyne leaped to her feet. "Did we not rule against the trifling with powers better left alone? And yet, when the Matriarch's ongoing meddling threatens to undo us, you warn her of our intentions to stop her? How is that *not* treason?"

Meryk rapped his stick upon the floor for order. "For years on end the position of Matriarch has become nothing more than a figurehead," insisted the First. "And with an untrained fledgling adept upon the Guardian's Seat, we are now the only true ruling power remaining to Eilar, the one light the people have in this coming darkness. It is the Council that has continued to keep our laws and traditions alive these many years. It is the Council that will continue to do so."

"You speak of tradition, yet you discount the heir to the bloodline?" Zoshia scoffed.

"That line is broken," First Councilor Meryk told her. The others nodded in agreement.

"But we have a Matriarch." Zoshia insisted.

"Do we?" someone asked.

"The ritual—"

"Was poorly performed," the First accused. "The oath I gave was not properly recited."

"The oath you gave was twisted," Zoshia exclaimed.

"It was made anew to serve the current needs of the people," the First shot back.

"But the binding is done," Zoshia said, glad now that she had not hesitated in her part. At least they could not take that away.

"Do not be so smug, Zoshia Valpine," Councillor Kendryn said as she stepped into the chamber. "What is done can be undone." She held up a heavy tome. "I have found the precedent you asked me to seek, Council First." She strode forward and placed the ancient book upon the table, opening it and leafing through its contents "Not simply precedent, but the exact means for the unbinding."

"No!" Zoshia shouted. "Other than death, the only way to unbind a sitting Matriarch would be to—"

"Rip her from the lines." Kendryn stabbed a finger at the page.

"But that will break her," Zoshia reached for the book, but strong hands restrained her.

"The needs of our people weigh more than the mind, or the life, of a single individual."

"Meryk. Do not do this!" Zoshia shouted, trying to look each of them in the eye, to make them understand how wrong they were. "Do you not see? It goes against our ways, against all we are."

Again, the First pounded the floor with his stick. "Zoshia Valpine," he intoned once the room had fallen silent. "You are formally removed as Second of this Council." He glared around at the rest of the Council members. "And I now call for a vote to rescind your appointment to the Council of Eilar and banish you from these chambers."

Around her, the voices of those whom she had debated with, sided with, and worked beside for years were raised in agreement as the two councilors who held her shoved her out of the chamber and into the rough hands of the Council guards.

* * *

Zoshia struggled against her captors. She needed to warn Devira of what was coming. Anyone still loyal to the Matriarch was now in dire jeopardy. Only the Council's focus on preparing for their present task and their belief in their own power and righteousness had kept them from enacting immediate punishment upon her. There was still time to warn them, to allow Kira the opportunity to offer to release herself from the binding. Though, Zoshia knew from all of their interactions how unlikely that would be. But she must try to convince her, make her understand that she would not be alone in her suffering if she refused.

"There is no need to restrain me," she said, trying to wrest herself from their hands.

"We answer to the Council," said the guard on her left, a tall woman with hard eyes and a mouth to match.

Zoshia stopped fighting them. "There is at least no reason to hurt me," she complained.

The guard on her other side simply grunted. Then, after a moment, he loosened his grip on her arm a bit, but nether guard made any move to release her.

The raised voices within the Council Chamber grew to a fevered pitch. Even though they had decided on a course of action, they would debate the timing and the approach for at least a few more hours. Or so she hoped. "I did not hear the Council order me detained. Merely removed." Zoshia squared her shoulders and regained the mien of Council Second. "And, as you can see, I have been removed."

The guards glanced at one another, uncertainty in their eyes.

"I may no longer be a Councillor," Zoshia told them. Her time on the Council had taught her something of debate and persuasion, after all. "But I remind you that I am still a free citizen." *Until the Council realizes their oversight.* "A free citizen, who by law may not be detained without cause."

First one and then the other released their grip on her. She straightened her robes, smoothing the fabric with shaking fingers, and attempting to calm herself. "Thank you." She held up her hands in the formal sign of respect before striding away. She forced her feet to carry her calmly out of the Council building, and begged her knees not to buckle, even as her mind continued spinning, spooling out the thread of what might be. Each scene played out before her, ending worse than the last.

For the first time since she could remember, hopelessness clawed its way into Zoshia, pushing out her confidence and filling her with despair. Even the Outlander attack during Kavyn's betrayal had not seemed as life ending as what was now happening.

What would become of them? What further damage to the land and its people would be wrought by this conflict between a bound Guardian and the Eilaran Council?

Not that the outcome of the struggle was in doubt. No one could stand against the might of the full Council. Not alone.

Chapter 51

As the shadow of his late night visitor receded into the darkness, Marquon sat at the tactics table eyeing the map of Eilar spread before him. He stood as Tesalin strode into the room.

"Was that the Council Second?" she asked.

Marquon glanced around to be sure they could not be overheard. "We have been tasked with a matter of grave import." He stepped around the table to close the distance between them and held out his hand in formal request. "I need your word that you will not share what I am about to say to you."

Tesalin rolled her eyes and gave him an exasperated look. "The last time you made me take such an oath, was—"

"We've no time to discuss my many past mistakes and shortcomings." He tilted his head and focused pointedly on his outstretched hand.

She blinked.

"This is not a game," Marquon said. "I assure you."

Tesalin's face grew deadly serious as she reached out and placed her palm against his. "My word."

He dropped his hand as relief washed over him. Now, all he needed to do was convince her to go along with him. Or, at the very least, not take up her sword against him.

Chapter 52

"Ho! Come quick!" Dahl shouted, standing in the corner of the cell as far as possible from where Milos gagged and retched spilling the contents of his stomach over the floor. "Guard!"

"Shut your jaw!" the Outlander shouted down the passageway.

"Help. I think he's dying!"

"Not that I care," said the man as he made his way toward them, the lamp he carried casting long shadows that swung back and forth with the rhythm of his gait. "But Ekzarn doesn't want his precious cargo spoilt. Especially, not this one. Not afore he's ready, anyway." He snickered, then stopped outside the cell and peered in. He took a sudden step back and stuck his hand in front of his face. "Oi! What is that stench?"

"I told you. He's sick. You need to let me out of here." Dahl gripped the bars of the cell in earnest.

"He don't look so bad." The man laughed. "As for you, you can swim in it for all I care."

Milos started to choke. He fell over on one side with a

thud.

Dahl leaned over him, then stepped back. "He's...he's not breathing."

"Spit and boils!" The guard stabbed a key into the door lock and wrenched it open. He prodded Milos with the toe of his boot and sneered as Milos let out another cough and rolled onto his back. "Not dead. Not yet, anyway."

"I think it's catching." Dahl said, skirting the big man and dodging out of the cell.

The guard grabbed for Dahl, but the boy was too fast. He ducked beneath the man's reach and scrambled up the passage toward the open hatch.

"Come back here, you rotter." The Outlander lunged after him.

Chapter 53

"We go where? To guard against what?!?" Tesalin bristled beside Marquon as they trotted through the night.

"You heard me." MHe gritted his teeth, straining to hear above their running feet whether they might be followed.

"Treason then, Marquon?"

"I thought you'd appreciate a bit of exercise." He carried his sword at the ready, in case they should encounter resistance, but the only sounds that disturbed the silent city were their own falling footsteps and harsh breathing against the chill of the fallen night.

"Hah," Tesalin huffed beside him. "Your idea of exercise—"

"Could kill a grown man. So you've said. But we swore an oath to protect Eilar, this land and its people, against all threats, though they may come from within—"

"I'm well aware of the oath we swore." Tesalin's tone made it clear she was unhappy with the course of their conversation.

"Then you should have no trouble defending Eilar even against the Council."

She stopped short. "But you are suggesting the Councilors have somehow become enemies of the state!"

Marquon had to double back to where she stood, her hands on her hips and her chest rising and falling with the shortness of breath caused by their run. "Not exactly enemies of the state," he said, panting. "But what they intend is wrong."

She crossed her arms and set her jaw.

"Just hear me out," he said.

"Fine." She settled into an impatient stance.

"On the way?" He gestured toward the Keep and took a tentative step, hoping she would follow.

Tesalin narrowed her eyes, but stepped up to stride beside him as he set a quick-march pace, thinking hard on what he might say to persuade her to stand with him.

There was a long silence during which they neared the Guardian's Keep and Tesalin slowed her gait.

He stopped and turned to her where she had paused in the shadows outside the open archway. "If you choose to go no farther, I will not fault you for it. But I will defend the Matriarch with the last ounce of skill and blood I have."

"The Matriarch," she all but spat the title. "This is why you placed command of the Guard in the hands of another. In order to relieve yourself of that responsibility and instead—what?—take the side of an alien interloper against our own Council?"

"If need be, yes." His conviction rang in his own ears, but until he had spoken the words aloud, he had been uncertain of their truth. Now, having sent them into the world, he knew exactly what he believed, and what he would die for. Though, it pained him to think that Tesalin, his closest friend and ally since too far back to even recall, might now become his foe.

She eyed him, squinting into the shadows, as if trying to read through him.

He opened his mind to her, dropping his mental shields,

allowing her to glimpse the truth of what he knew in his heart.

She started, pulling away before she fell too far forward and discovered things that were better left unknown between lifelong friends. "Very well," she sighed. "I will stand with you."

He grinned in the darkness, preparing to move forward, but she laid a hand on his arm. "But if this goes bad for us," she grumbled in that way she had of making him know that she meant what she said, "I'll make certain you live to regret it."

"Well, then," Marquon raised his blade in salute, and it caught a flash of starlight. "Business as usual?"

He could sense her tight grin as they slipped forward through the dark garden and quietly breached the door, only to find it unguarded.

"Something is amiss," Marquon peered down the main hallway where most of the illumin-crystals had been dimmed to save energy through the quiet night, attempting to discern what might be waiting for them ahead.

"I agree," Tesalin said, "but I think it has to do more with your plan than anything else."

"Don't you think it odd that, after all that has happened, the side door to the Guardian's Keep is suddenly left unlocked and unguarded?"

"More like someone is sleeping at their post."

Marquon turned his attention to where Tesalin indicated and saw the watcher slouched against the wall, chest rising and falling in deep slumber.

Tesalin stepped closer to the sleeping guard, and drew back her foot, preparing nudge the man's boot with her own, but Marquon stopped her with a touch to her arm. "Let him sleep," he told her. "It makes our entry easier." He peered closer at the sleeping form. "Besides, this sleep does not seem natural to me."

"Drugged?" Tesalin peered around, searching for the

possible source.

"Or skilled." Marquon gave voice to the unsettling thought. That someone might use their skills for such a thing without consent went against their strictest laws. It was not an act that would be undertaken lightly.

"Whoever did so, is here with a purpose." Tesalin stepped away from the watcher, head whipping from side to side. "I'll cut anyone who dares to skill me," she grumbled low in her throat. "Never again."

Marquon shuddered, recalling the dark day when Tesalin's older brother had attempted to convince her to reveal her thoughts, trying to find out how much she'd heard between him and his friends about their plans to gamble their fathers' finest horses against one another in a wild race. She'd grown angry at his persistence and, when he tried to force his will upon her, she'd shoved him so hard, that when he fell back against the family's memory keep, he'd been knocked unconscious. She'd been a mere nine years old at the time.

Her stubbornness could make her a difficult friend, but it was also a part of her strength and made her a formidable warrior, and Marquon was glad she'd once again fallen on the side of ally, rather than foe.

The sound of raised voices drew their attention. In the distance, a group of Councilors strode toward the keep.

"Looks like you were right to be concerned," Tesalin said. "I've never seen so many members of the Council out in force like that. At least not for anything less than a formal transition or celebration."

"And the recent Inquiry," Marquon reminded her.

Tesalin squinted in the direction of the Council members. "And they're not in the mood for a party."

"Agreed. Looks like they're headed for trouble."

"More like they're planning to *make* trouble." Tesalin's face grew hard. "The Guardian's Chamber?"

"Indeed." Marquon ran for the stairs. *What am I getting*

us into, this time? His worry pounded at him in time with his racing heart as Tesalin followed him up.

Chapter 54

The Eilaran skilled went to work. In a few short moments, the cells were unlocked. The work of loosening the boards of the ship's hull that had been begun days before was set to in earnest and what had begun as seepage turned into full-on leaking. It wouldn't be long before the ship would be floundering.

"It's not the best plan to swamp the ship while we're still aboard," one of them said.

"I'd rather we didn't have to," Milos agreed, "but we need the Aestron crew occupied. And there's nothing they'll work harder at then to save their own skins. They've more than proven that." He rubbed at his shoulders where the marks of the ropes showed through his torn shirt as dark welts against his skin.

There was noise at the far end of the passage as the Outlander guard caught his prey and began to thrash him. He raised his arm to club Dahl with the small cudgel, but his forward motion was stopped when a firm hand gripped his wrist and twisted it hard. The weapon he'd been about to slam into Dahl's head was wrenched from his fist and used against him. He slipped to the deck, cracking his head against a beam on the way down.

"That's going to hurt when he wakes up," Dahl said, rubbing at his cheek where the man had managed to cuff him. He hauled back and gave the man a kick to his ribs. "Really hurt."

Milos put a hand out to keep the boy from giving the unconscious man another kick. "Save your strength," Milos said. "And your anger. You're going to need it before the night has worn to day. We're fighting for our lives. Don't think they'll offer us any mercy, if we lose. Understand?"

Dahl bit his lip and nodded.

"Good, now grab his weapons and keys and help me lock him in." He tied the man's hands behind his back, then tore off the tail of his shirt and stuffed it into his mouth.

Chapter 55

Marquon led the way, following the main passages but keeping to the shadows Several more watchers lay unconscious in the hallways. Every one had been skilled into deep slumber.

"I don't like it," Tesalin whispered.

"Nor do I."

Raised voices reached them, echoing off the stone walls.

Marquon paused and signaled for Tesalin to wait as he slipped ahead to peer around a corner. What he saw made him freeze in place a moment before easing back to where she waited.

She opened her mouth to speak, but he put a finger to his lips and waved her back the way they had come.

"What is it?" she asked in a low voice once they had moved far enough away to avoid being overheard.

"Councilors," he said. "It appears they are gathering for a confrontation, just as the Second warned me."

Tesalin's face grew hard. "The unconscious watchers?"

"Probably tried to halt them."

"That's a step too far," Tesalin's anger seethed. "The

Council should know better."

"Agreed." Marquon rubbed a hand across his face.

"What now? We cannot face the entire Council." Tesalin patted her weapon. "Nor do I wish to use this against our own people. Skilled or no."

Marquon quirked an eyebrow at her. "It appears my recent position as Head of the Protectorate is about to pay."

She narrowed her eyes in suspicion. "What do you mean?"

"I mean," he said, pulling a key from inside his tunic, "there is another way into the Guardian's Room."

Chapter 56

The Eilaran crept above decks, keeping to the shadows. A pale sliver of moon hung low in the sky. Where are the marines? Milos wondered, when a shadow rose up before him.

"What are you doing on deck?" a gravelly voiced man said. He opened his mouth to shout for his comrades, but something struck him hard against the side of his head. He fell forward onto Milos, who caught him and let him down slowly onto the deck so as to make as little noise as possible.

Dahl held up the cudgel and grinned in the moonlight. Milos picked up the man's sword.

They made their way to the small boats, launching the two closest to the bow. The water and wood skilled Eilaran set out to scuttle as many of the other ships as possible. The remaining few Eilaran had gone after their weapons.

Milos had finally convinced Dahl to clamber into one of the remaining boats, when there was a shout from above. The night watch had finally sighted them. Suddenly, there was scuffling and fighting all around them

Milos stared out across the dark water where Eilar lay. Eilar and Kira. He hoped against hope that her recent visitations were as real as he believed and not merely the hopeful dreams of a love-stricken fool. Either way, the threat Ekzarn posed to her and the Eilaran people was very real. "I don't suppose you would take a boat on your own while we clean up here?" he asked.

Dahl shook his head. "I've got work to do." He held up the heavy cudgel with two hands.

Milos sighed, then turned in time to dodge the arc of a heavy sword that sliced through the air, attempting to separate his head from his shoulders.

Milos reached for the coil of rope near the boats and hurled it at his attacker. It tangled around the man's sword arm, weighing it down. Milos stepped forward and punched the man hard in the temple before he could get his sword up.

"Quick, scuttle the rest of those small boats," Milos told Dahl. "Save these three."

Dahl slipped behind Milos to clamber along the rail and do as he was asked.

An angry roar erupted and Milos spun around to face Stronar. "I've been waiting for a chance to pay you your due," Stronar said, raising his weapon.

"And I to return all of your recent favors." Milos planted his feet and brought his sword to the ready.

The mate closed on him. "You'll be ever so grateful to know I intend to clear your debt." He slashed at Milos.

Stronar was roughly trained and Milos was the more well-practiced swordsman, but his recent days with little water and his even more recent sickness slowed his movements. The mate had him on the defensive in a matter of moments. It was all he could do to block and parry Stornar's angry, awkward thrusts and jabs while keeping outside the big man's cutting zone.

"The ship is sinking!" The shout from below made the

mate pause in his attack. Milos had hoped the sinking ship would become the entire crew's first priority, but Stronar only renewed his attack. "You'd sink us again?" he snarled, his anger palpable. "You'd finish what you and your witch started?"

Milos bore the brunt of the man's angry frenzy. A lucky blow bit into his forearm and blood coursed from the wound. He hadn't much time, the blood loss along with his physical weakness would turn the fight in the mate's favor in short order, and the big man showed no sign of his rage-induced energy flagging.

Behind the mate a bloom of fire blossomed.

"Fire!" shouted one of the Outlander crewmen.

Stronar twitched his head to see, leaving himself open. Milos ducked inside, the tip of his blade slicing an arc across the mate's torso before he could recover. Stronar pulled back and placed his offhand against his chest. It came away dark and wet. For the first time, his face showed doubt and Milos knew he had finally gained the upper hand. He wasted no time on the fire nor the fighting that had erupted around him, attacking with the last of his energy.

He pressed the mate back. Then, with a sudden jerk, he sent the Stronar's blade spinning across the deck. The mate howled in frustration. Then he turned and ran.

Milos didn't have the strength to pursue him. Besides, his objective lay in the captain's cabin.

Chapter 57

"I always wanted to spend time in the Guardian's Room," Tesalin said, dragging another granite stand over to the doors, where Marquon leaned against the growing pile of items. "Though, this was not the way I imagined it."

Marquon peered at the heavy doors and the makeshift barricade. "I don't suppose they might give up?" He repositioned himself to get better leverage against the furniture they'd managed to shove up against the thick oak doors.

"I don't expect so." Tesalin pushed against another statue, toppling it from its stand. She pursed her lips together and eyed the broken form. "There are still stone adepts who are able to work with...with whatever this is made from, I suppose."

"Probably." Marquon frowned. "I think it best to give them plenty to do."

She braced her back against the heavy stand and inched it over to the door. "If...you'd lend a hand...rather than standing...around...that might be arranged." Her words came out as a series of grunts over the scraping of stone against stone as she pushed the stand over to where Marquon stood watching her. He gave her his best grin before shifting forward to help. Together, they shoved it against the rest of the items they'd used to create a barricade, then leaned against the pile of assorted furnishings, panting from the exertion. Across the room, to the rear of the dais, the back way had already been barricaded. "Too bad about the first consort's statue," he said, thinking of the exquisite figure they had tumbled from its plinth to block the entry.

Tesalin gave him a wry smile. "A bit late to admire the workmanship, now." After a moment, she stepped away from the barricade and jutted her chin at the heavy doors. "It's grown quiet." Her hand went to her weapon, where her palm rested against the pommel, fingers lightly curling around it. "Do you think they'll attempt to challenge the Matriarch through all of this?"

"Doubtful. I expect they'll be fetching those adepts you mentioned. Possibly movers. Antor's daughters can manage that sort of shifting through walls when they work together. Though it will take time and effort for them to move this much." Marquon waved at the blockade of furniture, dusted his hands on his trousers and surveyed the wreckage of the room. He looked pointedly at Tesalin's hand on her hilt. "That's not going to be much help."

"Nor, as I said before, would I ever wish to use it against any of our own people. At least not in a real fight." She gave him a weak smile, but didn't take her hand away. "Though, it's become a familiar bit of comfort of late."

Marquon knew what she meant. The drilling and sparring, working side by side, the act of letting one's mind share outward with others who, like them, were focused on the protection of their land and their people, these things had indeed become a comfort. The Eilaran Protectorate had become more than a group of soldiers, they had become as close as blood kin. Their weapons had become more than tools. They represented a connection with like-minded individuals, an extension of self as part of a larger whole. Sisters and brothers in arms. He wished them well, hoping the quiet outside the doors did not mean they were being summoned to fight against their founder. He shot a look at Tesalin and once more wondered what he had gotten them drawn into.

Up on the dais, the dual-adept, Aertine, stood with a small group of skilled. He considered the connection they sought to create and shivered.

Tesalin saw where his thoughts lay. "Interesting what changes in alliances have come to pass with the return of the Matriarch's heir and her rise to power."

He shrugged. Did these allies know what powers they were dealing with? What changes the meddling with such things might bring to their already changing land?

And what of the power he could already feel spilling over into the chamber? Was it anchored somehow to the island in the same way their Matriarch was chained to the Guardians' seat through the binding ritual? Would the ties they were attempting to make with the dark stone Mistra Aertine had created bind them all? He'd never been inclined to travel—at least not before Milos had talked him into to agreeing to cross the sea to escort his stallion to Aestron next season, a trip that was already now in question—but the thought of being permanently chained to a place, even to his beloved homeland, caused a shiver of revulsion to wash through him. He hoped his friend would understand if he was unable now to keep his promise.

Beyond them, Matriarch Kira, sat upon the Guardian's seat. Beside her stood a small group of Physics led by her personal Physica, Devira. And yet, she was mated to the Council Second. Strange alliances, indeed.

If Marquon weren't here now himself, defending this Matriarch from the Council's interference, he might find it all quite unbelievable. But there was something about this Matriarch. There was a magnetism about her. Perhaps it was her dedication, or her lack of arrogance, but Marquon sensed that this woman was not seated here on the Guardian's seat for any other reason than the defense of Eilar and its people.

"Do you know what they're about?" Tesalin's question broke into his thoughts.

"Only that they seek to help connect the Matriarch with that ugly piece of work. Something to do with the lines of power and protection of Eilar. Though, there seems to be more they refuse to say." He shrugged. "I'm only a defender."

"My goal is to protect," Tesalin intoned, finishing the Protectorate's mantra.

They gazed up at the activity taking place on the dais. Mistra Aertine, and her apprentice—Marquon searched his memory for the young man's name, but couldn't quite find it—stood on either side of the strange stone, intently focused. Whatever it was they were attempting, was taxing them both to the extreme. Even from this distance, Marquon could make out the beads of sweat that ran down the sides of the young man's face. His shirt was damp and the Mistra's hands shook with the effort of their task.

The fist-sized stone that sat before the Guardian's seat was multifaceted. Light seemed to emanate from it, but in a strange flickering pattern rather than the steady aura of a typical illumin-crystal. And, unlike most of the stones and crystals used for light and heat, within the light that shone from it, the stone itself appeared black, as if it somehow contained the dark of night.

The group of adepts and skilled gathered around the Matriarch and the odd stone were so absorbed in their work, they hadn't seemed to noticed the scraping of stone and wood against the marble floor as Marquon and Tesalin barricaded the door, much less the heavy pounding of those outside attempting to break in. Nor the ominousness of the deepening quiet that had filled the room since it had stopped.

Marquon studied the great doors against which they had piled as much stone and wood as possible. "To be fair. I'm more concerned about what those gathered on the other side of these doors might be planning."

Chapter 58

The airslingers worked in unison, attempting to smother the fire. Smoke curled up into the sky and smoldering bits of sailcloth fell onto the deck of the ship as the flames slowly dampened and died.

A few scattered fights continued, though the Eilarans seemed to have won the advantage.

Milos skirted the melee and rushed to meet his quarry nearly running into the big man guarding the door.

"I was hoping we'd meet again," the marine said, swinging his sword down and across, in an attempt to reach past Milos's blade. But though the man's reach was longer, Milos was too close to his goal to be held back now. He dodged out of range, the tip of his opponent's blade barely missing his throat.

Rather than hiding his exhaustion, Milos smiled and locked eyes with the man, letting his sword tip droop a fraction. His body was ready to succumb to his torments and lack of sleep and nourishment. He stood his ground by will alone. But will would need to serve. "Unusual to wish for one's own death." He let the words trail out, as if there were no conviction behind them.

The Outlander grinned as his eyes flicked to Milos's sword point. He snarled and lunged forward, thrusting his blade at the opening.

Milos faded to the side, keeping his movements as modest as possible without putting himself within his enemy's striking distance.

The marine shifted his stance. "You may as well give up. You're already exhausted. As good as dead." He took a step forward.

Milos retreated a step, but wasted no breath on a response. One thing he'd learned from sparring with Marquon's guard was that talking was a waste of precious energy. And Milos had none to spare.

The marine closed on him, his blade glinting in the moonlight as he struck.

Each blow Milos deflected felt heavier and more fierce than the last, a sign of his flagging strength.

"It's but a matter of time." The marine danced from side to side, in a show of prowess.

Milos tried to watch the man's entire body, but he was losing focus. The Outlander was right, he wouldn't last much longer.

His opponent struck again, leaping forward and putting all his weight behind the assault.

Once more, Milos dodged, but his wavering strength betrayed him and he found himself within reach of his foe.

The marine saw it, too. Only the flicker of his glance gave away his intent a mere moment before he swung his weapon again.

Milos barely twisted away in time to dodge a direct hit. The sting of slicing blade ran fire across the left side of his ribcage. But the marine had been so sure of his blow, he'd left himself within range. With the last of his waning energy, Milos drove forward and slashed downward. His blade ripped through the man's leather jerkin and into the hard muscle of his left thigh. Though not a killing blow, the cut was deep.

Blood streaked Milos' blade as he fell back. He ducked and leaned to the right, as his enemy swung his sword in an arc attempting to make contact even as his left leg tried to give way under his weight. Red seeped out and stained the man's pant leg

"Surrender," Milos said, "while the Physics might still save you."

"None of their demon magic will ever touch me." The big man gnashed his teeth against the pain, putting his weight on his right leg as blood ran from his left to stain the deck. He pointed the tip of his sword at Milos's throat. "But I will take you to the other side of the gate with me where I can kill you again and again for sport."

Milos shook his head at the Outlander's odd beliefs. If they both fell to the wheel this day, their journeys might possibly be tied in some way, but the wheel was not a place where personal scores might be settled. He kept his distance as fresh blood pooled at the man's feet, darkening the deck.

The Outlander's breath quickly grew labored. No surprise with the loss of blood. Milos was beginning to feel the effects of his own wounds. The man would shortly lose consciousness. Milos merely needed to wait him out. If he could. He retreated another step to add some distance between them but, as he did, his opponent let out a roar and attacked again, stumbling forward and teetering sideways as his left leg refused to bear his weight. Milos barely managed to parry the man's blow and duck aside. His months of heavy training taking over, he stepped into the man and thrust his blade into his midsection, pulled it out and stumbled away before his foe could recover.

The Outlander went down onto his right knee, then fell against the outside wall of the captain's cabin, coughing blood. His eyes glazed over and he toppled to the deck.

Milos kicked aside the man's blade and reached for the door handle. It was time to put an end to all of this killing and dying. It was time to put an end to Ekzarn and his continuing threat to Eilar. And Kira.

He opened the door and stepped inside. The cabin was dimly lit by a single lantern that hung from the overhead beams.

Milos slashed his blade across the bedding in frustration, then leaned against the wall, staring around at the empty cabin.

Chapter 59

Ekzarn clutched the head of his walking stick and stared across the water at his homeland. Finally! He'd waited too long for this day. Lost too much in the process.

"What orders for the assault?" the Outlander Marine bristling at his side asked.

"Just keep them busy," Ekzarn told him, his impatience showing as he stepped onto the waiting boat. "Now that they have remade the stone, I need only to set foot upon the shore to gain the power to wrest control from their inept Matriarch." *And claim what is mine.*

The Outlanders rowed quietly away from the armada's armed vessels, which continued to barrage the port with dragon's fire. A single small boat, launched from the away side of the closest ship, unnoticed amid the confusion and chaos their attack created. They could slip southward and find their way into the mouth of the river that would lead them directly into the heart of the city. And from there, it would be a simple matter of entering the Guardian's Keep. And anyone who dared to get in his way would be annihilated.

He smiled to himself in the darkness, sensing the power that would soon be his. It called to him, urging him forward as oily flames streaked the sky overhead before falling to earth to set the Eilaran port ablaze.

Chapter 60

Kira stretched her reach, pulling at the threads of power, braiding them into a taut line and finding some semblance of the energy she needed to hold on, to fight against the strength of the entire Eilar Council. No, she reminded herself, not the entire Council. In the end, Zoshia had finally been persuaded to side with them, had even managed to send them aid. Though, it was only her love for Devira that had finally turned her to their side.

Love, the word dragged at her like a sucking tide, and it was all she could do not to lose focus and have her grip on the power wrenched away.

The voices in her head rose up in waves, "You know not what you do." "You must stop."

"Give in," one especially low voice called to her. "Let go. Your freedom is merely a moment away." It cajoled and soothed. There was something magnetic about it; the way the words wove hypnotically in and out of the others, making them seem point and counterpoint, like a familiar lullaby.

"Kira," Devira's voice cut through the mesmerizing tune.

"We are here with you."

She yanked her attention back to her task, pulled and braided another line, then wo
ve the lines together. The land lay poised, tensed, the energy lines taut and humming. The chains of power anchored her as the energy pushed and pulled her like a buffeting wind. The urge to shove off the heavy chains and let herself be pulled into the stormy fray of power never left her, but it was a lure she must resist.

The power stone that Aertine had created pulsed in Kira's fist as she pulled the lines of energy to it, tying them off one by one. The Guardian's room thrummed, the walls echoing back the resonance of the building power. She only wished she knew that what she was doing was right, that it was the answer to saving them all. But there were no guides here, no mentors to offer their wisdom. Nothing but her instincts and the part of her she had so recently learned to trust once more.

The cold of the Guardian's seat seeped into her, the hard stone seemingly intent on melding with muscle and bone. The fear of the Council was palpable. It washed over her, even as she pulled yet another rope of power and tied it to the stone.

She needed to complete this task, but time was running out. Her strength was ebbing low. Where now was the great gift that the Matriarch had endowed upon her? Where was the power she needed to save these people despite their desire to destroy her?

Aertine's words came back to her. "I've no idea if it will hold to your purpose. The Pillars, they were made to withstand much, but this?" She had eyed her repair work with uncertainty. "I cannot promise," she'd admitted as she'd handed the patched-together gem to Kira.

And, as Kira had taken it from her, a sense of dread had fallen over her. The sensation that everything was destined to change. And not for the better.

She'd shooed the thought away, as one would an annoying insect, but it had continued to buzz in her ear and, even now, it would not let her be.

She settled herself and held the stone before her, opened herself further to the lines of power that connected her to Eilar and began dropping her shields enough to seek the keystone's core.

Chapter 61

Ekzarn sloshed ashore. The moment his feet came into contact with the land of his birth, his strength returned and the land's energy rose through him, filling him with power. For the first time in years, he wanted to laugh out loud. Tears of joy burned at the corners of his eyes, as he strode away from the beach where they'd landed, but there would be time for celebration later. For now, he had a country to wrest from the hands of its weakling Matriarch.

His men followed warily, glancing nervously over their shoulders as if expecting a monster to jump out at them from the evening shadows. He could have put their minds at ease, but why bother? They were no longer necessary and would be useful only if they ran into resistance. He rolled his head and cracked the bones in his neck, loosening the pressure that had come to reside there since his ousting from this shore. He opened his senses wide.

The closer he drew to the Guardian's keep, the more elated he became. His spine straightened and his muscles became infused with energy. "Now, this is what I call a homecoming." He laughed and, as they approached the keep, tossed aside his useless walking stick, glad to be finally free of the ridiculous crutch he'd been forced to use. His men traded furtive glances that he sensed rather than saw. In fact, his senses had come alive. His skin hummed with power.

They neared the keep and he slowed his stride. Up ahead, an undercurrent of anxiousness and anger flowed out to greet him. He signaled his men to stop moving and stood still, allowing himself a moment to assess the situation. "What rare treat is this?" he murmured, licking his lips and savoring the taste of chaos. "Have we stumbled upon a land in strife?" With an abrupt wave of his hand, he sent four of his men forward. "Take the front stairs, circle left and head for the Guardian's room as I showed it to you on the map. Clear the way. Whatever means necessary." The men saluted him and moved quickly but quietly across the gardens. He squared his shoulders and gestured for the three other men to follow him. "I know another way in."

Chapter 62

"Something is terribly amiss." Marquon cocked an ear toward the hallway on the other side of the massive doors. Outside the room, a new commotion arose. The stomping of feet and the sound of something heavy being thrown was soon drowned out by shouting and the cry of, "Outlanders!"

"To me," someone called out above the tumult. "Shielders!"

"What—?" Tesalin's question was cut off by more shouting and screams coming from outside the room.

Up on the dais, the gathered adepts paused to turn and look as chaos erupted out in the hallway.

"Hells!" Marquon cursed and began shoving aside the barricade. "We have to help them."

* * *

The three Outlanders heaved at the door, but it wouldn't budge.

Ekzarn grew impatient. "Are you truly so useless?"

One of the men opened his mouth to respond, but

before the words could form in his throat, Ekzarn raised a fist in the air and the door and everything that had been blocking it from the other side, shattered. Debris and dust filled the air. Ekzarn's men shouted in surprise as one of their comrades was tossed aside and crushed beneath the midsection of a marble statue of an ancient consort. One of the Outlanders moved to help his comrade, but Ekzarn waved him off. "Never cared for either of them," Ekzarn said eyeing the broken man beneath the statue's rubble. He wiped the dust from his sleeves and strode through the doorway and up the narrow access steps that led to the rear of the Guardian's dais.

* * *

Tesalin had already moved into action, working frantically beside Marquon to clear a path to the door when the rear of the chamber erupted.

Up on the dais, the adepts surrounding Kira, held their positions, their faces strained. A few covered their heads or ducked as shards of stone rained down on everyone, but quickly resumed their positions.

Tesalin and Marquon drew their swords and turned in time to face the men who climbed the backstairs to the dais. While from out in the hallway came screams, men and women, fighting, dying. Marquon cursed the Outlanders and their unseemly timing. Cursed his own absence from his guard. Hoped they had been called to aid in the fight against the invaders. Prayed to the ancestors they would arrive in time to help those outside.

Two Outlanders and a tall fair man paused to take in their surroundings. Tesalin and Marquon charged forward and the Outlanders met them midway.

Devira gasped. "Ekzarn!"

"Curse the ancestors, the charwoman is still alive." Ekzarn sneered.

Aertine jerked her head up, anger coloring her features, but Devira shook her head and whispered quietly. "Focus on doing what needs doing," she told her.

Her sister gave her a worried look, but bent back to the task of helping Kira to gather the strands of the land's energy into a coiled rope.

The Physica placed herself between Ekzarn and Kira. "Once more, you bring violence to this place. Will you never learn?"

He glanced at the melee of sword slashes and shrugged. "A little bloodshed will simply brighten up the place and make it more like home."

"This was never your home," Devira told him.

"I'm not here to discuss your rigid social strictures regarding bloodlines and ancestry, old woman." Ekzarn peered over at Kira and the adepts surrounding her. His eyes glinted brightly as he caught sight of the focus stone. He pointed at the gem. "But that belongs to me."

Chapter 63

The door began to open and Milos raised his sword point, though he had no more strength to wield the weapon. If the person on the other side of the door was a foe, it would be a short fight, but he would do his best to not be easily overcome.

"Milos?" Dahl poked his head inside.

Relieved at the sight of the boy, Milos let the sword tip drop to the deck, where it struck a splintering gash in the planking. "The fighting?" he asked.

"We've won the ship." Dahl slipped inside, glancing around the room. "But the flagship has disappeared. Along with most of the others. The Eilaran crew have all come back aboard."

Discouraged and exhausted, Milos sank down into a padded chair and leaned his weapon against the bulkhead. "What of the Aestron sailors?'

"First Mate Stronar survived." Dahl glanced down at the deck before continuing. "He and a few others... I couldn't stop them. They took the remaining small boats."

"Fools." Milos shook his head. "They're too far from

land. It's unlikely they'll survive."

"It would serve them right. If it were true." Dahl rubbed the back of his head and winced.

Milos finally noticed the boy was no longer holding the cudgel he'd taken in the earlier fighting. "Are you hurt?" Milos started to rise.

"I'm fine," Dahl said, trying to reassure him. "And the fires are out, but...there's more."

"More?"

Dahl shook his head. "We aren't that far from shore. The captain says we're not far from Eilar. And...there are flames."

"But you said the fires were out." Milos used the heavy sword to help himself stand.

"The ship is no longer burning, but there is fire in the distance. The Eilaran say the Outlanders are attacking Eilar."

"Kira!" A fresh purpose filled Milos as he rushed out onto the deck.

Chapter 64

Ekzarn strode across the room, careless of the fighting between the Outlanders and Eilarans. The power of the land buzzed through him, and the focus stone pulled at him. Perhaps, he should have brought more men. Then again, while the appearance of capable fighters had been a surprise, there were only two defenders here. And the rest of the Eilarans in the room, skilled or otherwise, would be no match for him once he held the key. His palms tingled with the need to hold the stone.

"You've grown even weaker than I'd hoped," he said, sensing the shifting focus of the adepts.

"Not so weak as to fall before you without a fight." The old Physica stood before him, her scarred hands raised as if they would help shield her.

He strode forward, stepping closer to the Guardian's seat and the convergence. Devira grabbed at his shirt with her withered hands, but he shook her off. "Be a good lapdog and heel, and I may find a use for you in my kingdom," he told her.

She stepped in his way once more. "Eilar will never bow

down to a man such as you."

He laughed, then knocked her aside with a sweep of his arm. The Matriarch was anchored in place, clumsily working the lines, a small number of adepts attempting to support her. "So, it's true," he gloated. "The untrained leading the undisciplined." He paused for a moment. He could not come at her physically, not while she sat upon the Guardian's seat. The shielding that had been placed on the seat was designed to protect the Guardian. But her lack of training would be her undoing. He merely had to come at her through the convergence. The keystone was his doorway, and she had already opened it.

This would be too easy.

A sudden sword was thrust between him and his prey. "Not all are untrained or undisciplined," the woman holding the blade growled.

She had bested one of his marines. The worthless man lay in a pool of blood while the other Outlander continued to battle the Eilaran warrior, the clashing of their swords ringing through the room.

Ekzarn glanced down at the tip of the blade she pointed at him and gave her a feral grin. "It seems the Eilarans have learned a few new tricks." He rolled his head, his neck bones cracking. "I've a few of my own." He opened up to the lines, wrested them away from the struggling adepts, one by one plucking the threads from their grip.

Their startled gasps distracted the swordswoman. She flicked a look over her shoulder at the sound. It was all the opening he needed to slam the power he'd drawn into her shields. She grimaced in pain, her empty hand going to her head as her sword hand wavered. He unsheathed his own sword and knocked her weapon aside. She stumbled back, raising her blade to block his attacks, but her movements were slow and his powerful onslaught continued until she stumbled backward down the dais steps, tumbling down, her sword clattering against the stone.

"Tesalin!" the Eilaran swordsman yelled.

Ekzarn turned in time to see the man running at him. The wounded Marine slumped against a pillar. "Must I do everything myself?" he muttered. He planted both feet and raised his arms, pulling glowing tendrils of power up before him. The writhing threads darkened as he wove them to his will. The man crashed into the wall of energy and fell back, his sword skittering across the stone floor. "Stay down," Ekzarn commanded as the man tried to rise. He sent tendrils of power slithering across the floor to pin the Eilarans in place.

He stormed across the dais and reached for the keystone. "No more playing."

Chapter 65

Kira struggled to maintain control of her thoughts. Her senses divided between what was happening all around her and her focus on shifting the energy, pulling it into place, reworking what was once a protective net for this island into something more offensive in nature. The cracks in the keystone caused the energy to shift and blur, making it difficult to keep a grip on the pattern she was weaving, strand by strand, into this new design.

The room had exploded behind her and the power dimmed. And now *he* was in the room. She could sense him, his hateful gaze raking at her like sharp talons. But she dared not look, could not allow herself to lose focus.

Ekzarn's voice grated against her skull, like the claws of a bear scraping against rock, scrabbling to get a hold that could be pried open far enough for ingress.

The weight of the Guardians' chains bore her down, as if they were an anchor and she a sinking ship. What had compelled her to this? To take this seat? To wear the chains of office? She was not of the—

Laughter erupted, exploding inside her brain and

suddenly she was drowning.

Dark shadows pushed at her thoughts. Every wrong thing, every bad choice, battered her. The whirling emotions that tore at her threatened to undo her concentration. Anger at what had happened to her father, and her mother. Fear of what might become of Milos and the growing life inside her. Guilt of killing Toril. Sorrow at the loss of her mentor, Heresta.

She had to shut it out. All of it. There was nothing but here and now. Nothing but the battle that raged. The battle that raged. Milos! No. She had to focus.

She was not drowning. She was here. Sitting upon the Guardians seat. Anchored by the weight of the Chains she wore around her neck. The chains she now knew were designed to keep her firmly tied to the physical plane. There was no way for her to pull away. No way to escape this onslaught. She had known he was coming. Known he would not stop until he took everything for himself. Knew that his fleet was already out in the harbor, burning and destroying. She could sense the pain of both people and land, the connection running deep. She'd tried to ignore it, tried to reach beyond the damage that was even now jabbing at her, bruising her soul and awakening the past, forcing her to relive the worst of Toril's brutality. She had vowed to protect this land and people from the fate of being brutalized by their own more powerful abuser. But he had arrived too soon. She'd had no time to rebuild the net, no time to shore up the defenses. And she had had no time to reconnect with Milos. No time to say the things she should have said.

Chapter 66

Milos sprinted for the main deck, Dahl at his heels. "Captain, we must head for the island."

"The Hawk is winged." Captain Jayvel gestured to the damage surrounding them. "Fewer than half her sails are intact. And my people are exhausted."

"But—"

"But we're doing all we can to get her underway." He placed a reassuring hand on Milos' shoulder. "We won't leave our people to be slaughtered, will we, Relten?"

"That we won't, Captain," Second Relten agreed.

Milos slumped against the railing, finally noticing the intense work going on around him. Sailors unfurling and tying off hastily repaired canvass. Adepts preparing to work the wind.

"Let me help you," the ship's Physic said. "There is time before we reach Eilaran waters."

Milos opened his mouth to argue, but his battle energy was spent and he felt utterly drained. He'd be of no worth in a fight in the shape he was in. He held up a hand and made the Eilaran sign of acceptance. "Thank you."

The Physic placed his hands over Milos' wounds, sending the familiar tingle of healing into muscle and tissue.

As his body mended, Milos watched the tiny sparks that fell across the dark sea and prayed to Troka the Eilaran Protectorate could hold back the tide of invaders and that they would arrive in time to help.

Chapter 67

Kira's grip on the lines shivered. The power was shifting away from her. She was trapped in a tug-of-war of power with Ekzarn, the land and its people strung upon the taut lines that stretched between them. She could not yield, yet she was losing ground. She could feel it in the way the ropy lines of energy slipped inexorably through her hands. Sensed it in the way he reveled.

Her head ached. Her body throbbed. Fire raced across her skin, and her fingers felt numb, like doughy loaves of unbaked bread, that refused to do her bidding any longer. Yet, she clung on with all her might, even as dark spots speckled the edges of her vision.

She was losing.

Memories rose up of her mother crossing the ocean in a tiny boat, leaving behind everything she knew in order to keep her child safe. Something shifted within her. It wasn't anger that drove its sharp talons into her now. Nor was it self-preservation. It was protectiveness. Her child would live. If she had to rip apart the entire Outland Navy and destroy every soldier they had sent at her people, her child would live.

She fought off the numbness, ignoring the fire, and yanked harder on the lines, pouring all she had into the making of not only shield, but weapon. With sudden insight, she let go of the strands of power, letting Ekzarn pull it toward himself with a mighty howl of victory. But before they slipped completely away, she lashed the ends of the lines to the stone, calling out to her island, to Aertine, to the people of Eilar to lend her their might.

Power once more surged through her, pulling the lines so taut between them they vibrated. With the added might of Aertine and the Eilarans, Kira sensed the tide shift.

Ekzarn shrieked at her, his voice hurling against her with as much force as the raging storm.

Sudden pain seared through her as the Chains of Office tightened around her neck. She reached a hand up to pull the gripping metal away from her throat, her breath coming in ragged jerks as the chains cut into her skin and squeezed tighter, but her hands seemed to belong to someone else. The dark spots once more crept into her sight, a fuzzy haze that blocked out her view, narrowing her vision.

Then Vaith and Kelmir were at her side. *No.* Kira told them. *Leave me. I told you to hide yourselves.*

But Kelmir leaped between her and Ekzarn and let out a roar of warning.

Vaith landed on her shoulder, clawing at the chains. He squawked in frustration at his inability to lift the heavy metal from her.

"So your pets prefer to die with you." Ekzarn sneered. "So courageous. I could put such bravery to use for myself. I'll just need you to remain conscious for a bit." He raised a hand, palm outward. The chains at her throat loosened enough for her to breathe.

Kira sucked in a wheezing breath and stared in awe as the threads that connected her to her beloved companions became visible, glowing with a silver light. She'd always known their connection was there, but had never seen it manifest in such a physical manner.

"Pretty, isn't it?" Ekzarn grinned. "This is going to hurt." Then he reached out a hand and grabbed the thread that floated between Kira and Kelmir, wrapped it around his fist and yanked.

Kelmir howled in pain and Kira felt a part of her ripping away. She tried to scream, but the chains were still tight against her throat. Vaith redoubled his efforts, clawing at the metal links.

Ekzarn laughed as he gripped the silver thread tighter. Kelmir struggled wildly, tried to leap at Ekzarn, but it seemed as if an invisible leash had been wrapped around him and held him at bay. Her companion's rage and pain filled Kira with dismay. Tears spilled from her eyes. "Let him go," she managed in a harsh whisper.

"I don't think so. But I will take the set." He grasped the thread that shone between Vaith and Kira. Once again, pain surged through her.

Vaith cried out, beating his small wings in an attempt to free himself from Ekzarn's grip.

No! A rage welled up in Kira beyond anything she had ever felt before. Anger so large it threatened to engulf her. She reached for the chains with renewed purpose. Her fingers scrabbled at the clasp that held the heavy burden and yanked it open. She pulled in a deep breath as she dragged the chains from around her neck, letting them fall to the floor in a jumbled heap.

The room misted, growing distant, as every line, every connection flared into focus. A prism of colored light filled the room. She tried to follow the threads that tied her to Vaith and Kelmir, tried to wrench them from Ekzarn's grip, but her body felt as if it were floating free. The swirling light made it impossible to focus. A quiet music wafted on the air. A peace she had not known before descended on her and she found herself melting into it, drifting away from everything. She watched, as if from afar, her reaching hand falling from the keystone, her fingertips slipping away from the patched gem. It would be so easy to let go.

Vaith shrieked in pain. *Kelmir, Vaith.* She gripped the keystone harder and forced herself to see through the glow of connections. There. Ekzarn was there almost right in front of her and he was pulling Vaith and Kelmir to him, prying open their minds, forcing them to let him in.

Kira tried once more to rip the connective strands from his grip, but he clung to them.

"They're mine, now." He grasped the glowing threads with both hands, pulling them into himself. Kelmir's claws scored the marble floor as he tried to reach Kira, fighting against Ekzarn's inexorable pull. Vaith fluttered like a dying butterfly as Ekzarn dragged him nearer.

Kira knew in that moment that there was nothing she could do to stop this. Nothing, except sever herself from her beloved companions. Her heart ached at the thought of the loss, the loneliness already filling up the space where they had always been. A part of who she was. But there was no other way to save them. No other way to let them live free.

She reached for the threads that connected them to her and sent her thoughts out to them. *I will always love you, my dear ones.* Behind the thought, she sent a wave of freeing energy, dissolving the threads, and her connection to Vaith and Kelmir. The glowing strands scattered into dust that sifted through Ekzarn's fingers, drifted into the air, shimmered and disappeared.

"No!" Ekzarn yelled, scrabbling at the glittering dust.

The rending pummeled her, the physical loss like being kicked by a horse again and again. It doubled her over.

Lost. Lost.

But they weren't lost. Vaith and Kelmir were still here, still beside her, panting, confused, but alive. Though she could no longer hear them, connect with them as she once had, they would live.

As would her child, and all of Eilar, if only she could do what needed doing.

Chapter 68

"Land ahead!" Dahl shouted from the lookout's position high above the main deck. His words floated down to where Milos stood at the railing, eyes glued to the horizon. The sloop had taken a beating, half of her sails had been destroyed by the fire and she limped along like a broken-winged gull. But they had finally reached Eilar.

Eilar lay before them. In their path lay the Outlander ships like a swarm of vultures and across the water stood the port city of the Guardian's Keep. Acrid smoke rose from flaming sections of the city, wafted across the water to sting his eyes.

His heartbeat quickened, chest tight with worry and fear for Kira and the Eilarans who at this moment fought to save their land and their loved ones. He needed to get ashore. Needed to help rout this foe.

"Are you well?" Sanden asked him.

"I'm fine," he said, hefting the sword he'd taken from the Outland marine.

"We all have loved ones who will be glad of our homecoming. If we can find a way to stop the attack." Her tone was grim.

Milos glared at the vile invaders' ships. Scuttling them now would only cut off the Outlanders' escape and give them even more cause to fight. Yet, there were too few small boats remaining to ship the Sun Hawk's entire crew ashore at once. "What will the captain do?" he asked.

Sanden glanced up at helm where the captain stood giving orders. "He'll get us as close to the fight as possible. But first, a few of us have dragon's fire to quench." She jerked her head in the direction of the ships hauling the trebuchets that continued to send a rain of fire onto the port city. "We could use another sword, if you're so inclined."

"Indeed." Milos eyed the burning city. Though, he'd rather be ashore, fighting side by side with Marquon and Kira. He gripped the hilt of his weapon as he joined the small group of Eilaran preparing to drop over the ship's side. Kira and Marquon were both capable warriors, he reminded himself. Right now, doing his part to stop the destruction of the city would at least help them on that front.

Chapter 69

Ekzarn cursed. Rage filled him. How dare she keep from him what he was owed! His destiny was to rule this land, to take what he wanted, to be given his due. He would not be denied.

He lunged forward and grabbed her, wrapping his hands around her neck. "The women of your line are all the same," he growled. "Always meddling. Always refusing. Always standing in the way."

She struggled, grabbing his wrists and kicking him, but he paid no heed. "You're too weak to rule."

He squeezed. Pleasure rose up in him at the sight of her reddening face, the way her eyes began to bulge.

Her knee came up and struck him in the groin. He doubled over at the sudden pain, releasing his grip on her. She spun away from him, reaching out for the keystone. He swung a fist into her back. She yelped and stumbled, and he hit her again. She fell to the floor.

He stood over her. "Now, you'll know your place." He swung his leg back to kick her, but his vision was blocked by leathery green wings as tiny talons ripped across his forehead. He swatted the creature with the back of his arm, sending it flying across the room.

He raised his leg again, but a burning pain struck as the Mooncat raked his claws down his thigh. A scream of wrath and pain loosed from him and he stumbled forward.

Chapter 70

Kira dragged herself across the floor and reached out with both hands, gripping the fallen keystone, gathered herself and pulled the energy of Eilar to her, striking at Ekzarn with a deep purpose, focusing all her might through the stone. The intense energy of dozens of minds collided into the gem, growing stronger as another and another of the skilled joined. Aertine and Varnon had done their part, using the stone to amplify their own abilities, reaching beyond the Guardians Room, gathering a multitude together to lend their skills to hers through the remade keystone.

The gem seemed to fluctuate in Kira's hand, as if taking a breath. There was a momentary calm, where everything dimmed and wavered before reforming into brighter focus.

Then the power exploded, scattering a shower of energy that radiated in his direction. Shards of it cut through him, driving deep. Light seemed to fill him and he screamed. His body blurred, shivered, shrunk into itself, then the light exploded outward with a shockwave that drove Kira hurtling through space, beyond light, beyond sound, beyond reach.

Chapter 71

Kira. The voice chided her toward waking.

Raven? Kira tried to speak, to voice her reluctance, her need to rest. It was too early for errands. She pushed away from the sound of her mentor, attempting to float away, once more.

You need to come back. You have responsibilities, now.

I'm so tired. Let me sleep but a little longer. Chores will wait until the light.

Kira! Wake up. Now!

Kira coughed and gasped. Her body ached in ways she'd never thought possible and her skin blazed with a fire hotter than the scalding bile of a basilisk. So, she thought, I have been punished, but I have survived. She drifted away, again.

"Matriarch?" Devira was by her side, as were several chanting Physics. The voices of the healers rose and fell as they murmured together, aligning their healing efforts.

Kira slit open her eyes. Light pierced her vision, sending tears running down the sides of her face. She tried to open her mouth to speak, but her salty lips were rubbery and her tongue clung to the roof of her mouth, as if stuck there. All that came from her was a mewling sound.

Gentle hands dabbed at her mouth with a wet cloth, dribbling moisture between her teeth. The cooling liquid, a tincture of herbs infused with something more powerful, burned as it contacted the wounds inside her mouth, then settled into a soothing balm as she swallowed.

Her blistered hands moved on the ends of uncooperative arms, as she tried to place them on her middle, to hug her unborn child and comfort her. Him?

"They are strong. They will be well." Devira's voice eased over her, growing and receding like the sound of ocean waves.

They? Kira's brain told her she must be delirious. Or dreaming. But the Physica's words and her heart beating in rhythm with two others told her the truth. Twins.

Vaith? Kel? Did you hear? Twins! But there was no response. She tried again, but she could not reach them. Panicked she sat up, only now recalling the strangling truth, remembering what had happened, as gentle hands restrained her and a quiet voice murmured, "I'm so sorry. So very sorry." Aertine's words echoed the sorrow and loss that welled up inside Kira as she reached for a connection. Any connection, only to find herself completely cut off. From everything. And everyone. Tears sprang to her eyes and she willed her mind to let her fall back into the numbing darkness and away from the horrible awareness of consciousness.

Chapter 72

"Remind me again why we are the ones clearing up this debris?" Marquon rolled another granite cylinder away from what remained of the makeshift blockade, then wiped his sweaty brow on his sleeve, leaving a dark streak.

"Perhaps, because it was we who made most of this mess in the first place?" Tesalin stood off to one side and surveyed the wreckage of the Guardian's Room. Broken statues and chunks of stone littered the floor. Displaced and overturned furnishings had been shoved against the walls to clear an open path in and out of the room.

"As I recall, I was offered no other options when I suggested the idea."

"Saying 'Help me shove this statue off and roll this plinth over to the door,' does not actually qualify as a suggestion. Nor, do I recall you asking for alternate proposals."

"You've always been so stuck on the details." Marquon said, unable to hide the laughter behind his words.

She hefted a large high-backed chair, righting it before sliding it closer to the wall.

"Thank you," he said quietly.

"For what?"

"Trusting me."

Tesalin grunted, but one corner of her mouth turned up in what was her best approximation of admitting he'd been right.

Chapter 73

"Matriarch—"

Kira's stern expression cut Zoshia off as she took the baby from Devira's arms and nestled her into her own.

Milos looked up sharply, body tensed as if for a fight, but he relaxed when Kira smiled at him.

"What?" she asked him.

"I was merely thinking how well motherhood suits you," he said.

Kira's face warmed. Motherhood was not something she had ever thought would 'suit her,' but her heart expanded each time she picked up one of her babes. Sometimes, she thought it might grow to bursting in her chest.

"So," Zoshia asked, "you intend to take your daughter and leave us in our time of disarray?"

Devira gave Zoshia a sharp look, but kept her thoughts to herself. Her Physic's duties precluded her from speaking out against an official representative of the Council, despite being lifemates, especially now that Zoshia had been elected to the role of First. Though, Kira knew the Physica and her lifemate were likely headed for another intense debate once they were alone that evening. Strong-willed couples. Well, that was certainly something she could understand.

"Children." Kira corrected her, repositioning the boy, who fussed and wriggled before falling quiet against her breast. "We have a son as well as a daughter, and they are equal in value." She breathed in the sweet milk smell of the child. "The Council may still be in some disarray as you put it, but the Eilaran will manage, even flourish, now that their best and brightest are not being lured to their deaths by a cruel and vengeful power monger." She glanced over to where Milos, holding Virina in his arms, hovered over the chancing board across from Aertine. "My mother's sister has seen to that."

Aertine didn't bother to respond, focusing intently on the game pieces and plotting out her next move. This version of chancing was new to her, but she had quickly picked up its tactics and had already become a fierce adversary for Milos. The new board and fine stone pieces she had gifted him glittered in the sunlight that cascaded through the open window. Kira couldn't help but marvel at how comfortable he appeared with their daughter in his arms and Dahl, who could barely be parted from him, sitting on a cushion beside him, watching his every move.

It was a vastly different view than that which had greeted her when she'd awakened in her chamber to find him beside her, still battered and bloodied from the battle that had raged upon the shores of Eilar. His face was drawn and he'd leaped to his feet as her eyes fluttered open.

"Is this a dream?" she'd asked, her voice rasping in her dry throat.

"No." Milos kneeled by the bed, grasped her hand in his and kissed her fingers, tears falling from his eyes. "Better than a dream."

"When I could no longer find you...no longer reach you...I thought I'd lost you, forever," she whispered, tears spilling from her own eyes.

"I couldn't let you risk it, anymore. Not once I believed the visitations were real."

"I'm so sorry about before. I thought—"

"Hush." He placed the back of his hand against her damp cheek. "I should have known your heart. That your thoughts, your actions, were only for—"

"Milos," she sat up and wrapped her arms around him, pulling him close so she could whisper into his ear. "I have something to tell you..."

"It will take years for our skilled to match the numbers of old. Perhaps, generations," Zoshia's complaining brought Kira back from her reverie. "What of the meantime? Would you leave us without a true Matriarch and Guardian?"

"You speak as if you are at risk of being invaded by the very people we have just quelled." Kira lifted Valden to her shoulder and gently patted his back, listening for the release of air.

"And who is to say we are not?"

"They have lost their leader and driving force and, I expect, their will for conquering."

"For the time being." Zoshia pushed her case. "But what of when they have finished licking their wounds and seek once more to reach another shore?"

"I have a feeling," Milos said offhandedly, moving a piece of blue quartz across the board and bumping off a spire-shaped bit of topaz, "having been rebuffed so heartily at the Aestron and Eilaran gates, they will seek elsewhere to expand their realm."

"But what if—"

"I will not live my life on what ifs and perchances," Kira told her, dangling a small wooden rattle before the baby, who gurgled his joy and reached for the toy. "You forget. By your own laws and traditions, I am no longer entitled to the title of Matriarch. Need I remind you that I am not even of the bloodline?"

Vaith flew in through the open window and soared

across the room to land on the back of Kira's chair. Valden shrieked in joy and reached for the small reptile. From his place in the sun, Kelmir twitched an ear toward the sound of the baby's mirth, but the big cat barely cracked a lid before settling back into restful sleep.

"But the bloodline has been severed." Marquon shifted in his seat and leaned forward, his posture reflecting the earnestness of his words.

"Not truly severed," Kira countered. "There is still Kavyn. Though I understand his condition worsens." Her gaze fixed on Devira.

"He is well tended by our most skilled," the Physica assured her. "But a broken mind needs the help of its owner to heal." She shook her head. "Kavyn is either unwilling, or unable."

"A new bloodline may be started. There is precedent." Marquon glanced over at Kira. "And who better than our current Matriarch and the heroic—"

"I believe we have already had this conversation." Milos gave his friend a glare that could cut stone, and Marquon's mouth closed tight.

"To be honest, I don't believe the Eilaran require a Matriarchal bloodline any longer." Kira set the rattle aside and raised Valden up for a better view of the glittering wyvern. Vaith eyed the baby, tilting his head one way and another, then settled himself just out of reach. "Consider what was accomplished when many minds worked together toward the same end."

"But we had you to guide us," Tesalin reminded her. She sat apart from them, arms folded across her chest as if afraid someone might offer to hand her one of the babies.

"And now you have the new warding stones as well as the keystone, which will allow the new Keepers to tap into them, if the rest of the Council approves the plan." Kira directed a look at Marquon. As the reinstated leader of the Eilaran Protectorate, he was now seated on the reformed

Council. A responsibility he had readily embraced.

Aertine's mouth curved up at the mention of her Guardian Stone replacements. "True, the Net is no longer as powerful as it once was, but with the creation of the new keystone, the warding stones are in their own way a reasonable defense, as long as the people work together."

"And you have the Eilaran Protectorate," Milos said, shushing quietly over Virina, who had begun to make a fuss.

Marquon leaned over and held out his arms. Reluctantly, Milos passed the child over to the big man, and gave his friend an exaggerated frown when the baby quickly quieted. Marquon shrugged and grinned. He stuck his forefinger out for the child, and she gripped it in her tiny hand, causing his grin to widen.

"But—" Zoshia stopped speaking at a light touch from Devira.

Kira smiled inwardly at the fresh intimacy between the two women. It was good to see them together, again. But she kept her voice stern. "I have waited long enough." Though nearly six moons had passed since that night, the pain of it was still fresh. While the birth of their children had soothed some of the hurt of her disconnection from Vaith and Kelmir, the wounding absence was still with her, would always be, despite the fact that her companions had stayed, refusing to leave her, even when she'd tried to set them free. Had her pain been their impetus for remaining? Would they one day leave her, after all?

She forced her thoughts away from such thinking. "Now, that the children are here and healthy, the Council can perform the unbinding without risking them harm." She recalled the pain of her disconnection with Vaith and Kelmir and wondered how much the severing of what remained of her connection to this land would cost her. But there was no time for such thinking. No value in worrying over what regrets she may have in the future. The sooner it was done, the less chance for her to change her mind. And the sooner she left Eilar, the better. And, perhaps, the cost would not be so great. Since the battle with Ekzarn and her unanchored time upon the Guardian's Seat, she'd spent little time in the Guardian's Room, other than to help guide the work of Aertine and the others. Already, her diminished connection echoed back at her in hollow measure with each and every footstep.

"You have my answer. The formal abdication will take place on the morrow. At which time, I will transfer what remains of the Matriarch's power into the new keystone, which will increase the warding stones' power." She glanced at Aertine, who acted as if she had nothing more on her mind beyond winning this round against Milos, but Kira knew better, recalling their hushed conversation from the previous day. The details of the remaking of the keystone would have to remain a secret due to the danger such knowledge might pose in the wrong hands. She pushed away the image of her brother, Kavyn, who still lolled and drooled in the House of Healing. "Aertine will guide the use of the new keystone."

"I've the skill to help you as you have asked," Aertine told her, "but I doubt the Council will ever accept my role as guide. Our sister, your mother—"

"Did what she did to save me."

"True, but there is also the matter of your bloodline," Aertine said it without ire, but Kira knew the cut went deep for her aunt. "There will be remnants of bitterness."

"You give people too little credit for seeing the truth when it is presented to them," Kira told her, hoping it was true. "The new Council has already accepted the truth of my birth, and that Matriarch Kyrina merely bequeathed her position and power to me." Despite some arguments that such a bequest from a clearly broken mind was questionable and should have been brought to the Council for deliberation and decision. "Besides, it will be my final decree as Matriarch. After all that has taken place, I think it will be embraced." Especially once they have opened themselves up to the memories that would be stored in the orb that had been installed outside the Guardian's room. Her parting gift to her mother's people would be the memories of her own story to this new Memory Keep. Just as she had added her childhood recollections of her mother, Ardea, to their family's newly erected Memory Keep.

She felt her heart expand, recalling the work Aertine and Devira had finally completed with the help of so many others. The tears of happiness she and her aunts had shared once the last strand of rescued memories had been woven back into the tapestry that made up their family history. Even with the few missing and tattered threads, there was so much that had been restored. So many memories to explore. So much that she would now not have the time to experience. For a moment, her resolve wavered. But one glance at Milos and their two babes was all it took to restore her commitment. Better to create her own memories.

"But there is so much more to do." Zoshia's voice brought her back to the moment.

"The first ship of the season will set sail for Aestron directly following the transition ceremony. And we will be on it. We will take our children home."

Milos smiled at her with an almost imperceptible nod of his head. She knew he was thinking of them riding with pride on Trad and Zharik back into Tem Hold, their babes carried safely in their arms. She had come to this land seeking her family's roots and discovered the branches of life's tree continued to grow, despite the loss of a limb. She nearly laughed aloud, wondering when she had begun creating her own Heresta-like wisdoms. It was clear her mentor would always be with her.

Vaith let out a squawk, as if reading her mind without a sending. *And you, too, my proud princeling,* she thought. *Though, we can no longer link our minds, both you and*

Kelmir will always be a part of me.

She smiled back at Milos and let her full senses open to their children.

Home, and the rest of our journey.

Together.

Acknowledgments

Thank you to my many readers for your patience in waiting for this book. I know you wanted it sooner, but we all wanted it to be right. I think it finally is.

SHARON SKINNER grew up in a small town in northern California where she spent her time reading books, making up plays and choreographing her own musicals (when she wasn't busy climbing trees and playing baseball.) She's been writing stories since the fourth grade, filling page after page with fantastical creatures, aliens, monsters and, of course, heroes.

She spent four years in the Navy, where she served aboard the first US ship to carry women to sea. She has also repaired laboratory and hospital equipment, worked as a warehouse production manager, telephone sales representative, professional trainer, visual information systems coordinator, grants professional and consultant. Somewhere along the way, she managed to obtain a B.A. in English and a Masters in Creative Writing from PRescott Collge.Her Young Adult and Middle-Grade novels tend to explore complex relationships, particularly those between mothers and daughters.

Still a voracious and eclectic reader, Sharon also loves drawing, arts and crafts, sewing, and costume-making (especially steampunk). Her guiltiest pleasure is online gaming, and her biggest weakness is home-made, double-dark chocolate fudge. She lives in Arizona with her husband and three annoying but lovable cats.

You can find her online at sharonskinner.com